NO M

Julie Reverb

Excerpts from NO MOON appeared in *The Quietus, Volume 1 Brooklyn* and *Gorse*.

Published by Calamari Archive, Inc.

New York—Rome

www.calamariarchive.com

For Dave

I WILL SAY THIS ONLY TWICE 7

THE OLD COUNTRY SPEAKS 8

I KNEW I'D BEEN BORN (a worse loss) 12

A PETTY DEATH 18

WHEN I WAS NOTHING BUT MOTION 20

CRIPPLE CABARET 22

DOWSER AT A BUSH FIRE (daddy) 28

BRANDING OUR FORGETTING (never odd or even) ... 34

BAD NEWS CIRCUS 39

NEWFANGLED UNCONSOLER 42

HID IN A WAD OF I 47

NULLEST; VOIDEST; DEADEST MEAT 57

THE WOMEN'S REGRET; THE MEN'S REGRET 60

INVERTED YEARNING 62

THE DANCES WE DID BETWEEN ROCKS AND HARD
PLACES 66

MATCHSTICKS AND THE SIZE OF THE DECEASED'S
EYES 84

THE PAIN WAS EVER NEW UNDER POURING VATS OF
SKY (burn unit) 96

Longing is the agony of the nearness of the distant
—Martin Heidegger

I WILL SAY THIS ONLY TWICE

I will say this only twice I want my porn tanned my Stockholm's to come with a smiling Singapore Grip I don't know names and how I'll make them out of letters that exist fresh retching is always a séance with memory in the worst of times I can see haircuts in moments I can knock their gait on a crooked table I don't know what I'm still doing here when they're breathing down my neck like this I'll find a seat by the door and ask for a strong drink for another dying thing there's a scathing moon with a dubious past outside it's all cruelty even in softest light is this tinnitus or an SOS there are back-alley ways of speaking and remembering

THE OLD COUNTRY SPEAKS

Ted's a bad god with a tight fist. My brother looks like him. The same severe parting and soot eyes. They say the mines fucked Ted's heart but it was gone before then. Gone before he got the boat and went down the pit and came back. Ted ended in a leaky stagger in a paddock's parched grass. A soft, puzzled muzzling. It wasn't his.

Cattle don't get enough credit. They have saints' eyes and can't bite.

Ted's bad bones hold up and rattle this house, his son Billy and his sisters. Flat Jesus above the fire looks away from the prime-time bruising galaxy. Ted's wife Jill has to sleep outside in the shed some nights, where the donkey brays and dreams. She sobs between winds that roll off the beach. She's too soft and sees good in everyone, or looks too hard for it when it's gone. Ted is too fond of the horses and comes home with no wages in mute red mists. Mum berates anything that breathes but will never hear a bad word said against a donkey. When I feel sad about mum I see donkeys.

I've seen black and white Jill with a chignon and veil and a mouth that's just said a tentative yes to a man in braces under a black shroud, conjuring ambulant light. She has creamy silent star beauty. A smooth nose that my dad's Roman side bulldozed.

She's polite with half-mast eyes, but this was before six weeks of sickness and cursing over rails. Before cynical sweeping of Chicago church steps. "Look at her look at her there she is," and a rush to the side to see that frigid green lady. Ghostbusters 2 made me think she was halfway to heaven. There in the rain she was a kid's tarantula scrawl. I felt blank, ready to mouth vomit into mist. I focused on the crystal drizzle that stuck to mum's perm, her dyed greys. We laughed and held onto her shyness that twitched in the way of large lenses. She was not confident in water; she could not swim. Which way would her shocked body jerk first? She is open-mouthed in the photos, younger, gazing higher like Jill whose hair kinked with the times. We are together on the hotel bed drunk dancing to Motown. She holds my wrist like when we crossed roads. I'm too old for that now. She forgets. A burial's what she wants.

I thought the skyscrapers would be tonguing the moon, onwards with deathless force. I wanted to be impaled by a chewy-voiced cop. I wanted to jaywalk. I did none of this.

Jill returned from Chicago to a crumbled man in a painted cake slab house, smaller portions and her parent's fresh graves. Chipped glass animals in display cabinets peeked and quaked. Shadow puppet excess across walls and Jesus speckled with last night's soup. Childish prayers whispered under blankets that heave-hoed til morning when bare feet slapped tired miles to school. "Mammy slept in the shed again. You didn't pray hard enough," said Billy with the dragging leg. The children would go on for longer the next night, rippling inside their chirping canon until the birds' dawn panic. The donkey also woke early, braying for reasons it soon forgot. The town knew Ted was a coward and Jill was too kind. The priest hit Billy for falling asleep in class.

I fell asleep with piano falling hopes. I confessed nothing.

Ted hammered the priest's mean pulse. He'd cottoned onto Billy's beating and the blind eye turning. The priest was a gummy one; the psalms whistled through his gaps in Mass. Nothing but the drone of phoning it in. Jill stayed quiet or didn't know.

"Ma, it hurts," Billy said in the tin bath while his sisters sponged his cuts. They'd sleepwalk into the same old ritual, pain binding them like antique feet. The boy will grow up to drink, to draw panopticon circles around himself with compass legs. He'll later climb stairs and hand over notes for damp, deep heat with women that aren't there.

The children trembled together while half-cut Ted did headstands in the snow, his upside-down face knowing full well any expedition was doomed. It was bad land, no good for farming. They'd perish here with him, he'd see to that. His young played along then trundled on under the gleam of night, Billy trailing, sad the birds wouldn't sing, not missing god or dad or Santee who never did anything for them anyway.

A close-up of my failed metamorphosis: my snatch is spineless, toothless, godless. My chilblained guilt doesn't last long but my grudges grin into the next ice age. I'm counting on it, you being here, our tea going cold together. This will be a lonely area for both of us.

A bloated body waits at the wake while drunk teens take keen turns to grope. They're supposed to be keeping watch of Ted tonight but refuse with blind skin, fingers sniffing for life and hid whiskey. A battleaxe aunt is delayed but will not hear of him moving before her arrival. She needn't worry: he lies seasick in his warm box for too long. It's a protracted, hulking business the children will never shake.

I KNEW I'D BEEN BORN (a worse loss)

Samsa and Merrick met my parents softly learnt me fingered my snatch in my narrow bed stars that glowed loud in the tar dark peeling pony sticker on my door mum did cold salmon as a starter dad kept asking the same question about the weather our teak seats creaked held together with glue clouds passed the windows and gawped my first words fuck the lot of yas

As a zygote, Lucy was facsimiled all of her later missed cues, her if onlys, her yawning wounds with grand designs. Suzuki and baby Mozart methodology had nothing on her mother's forward planning; her knowingness of life as a last resort. This is what it is to be prized.

Lucy still lived at home with her parents and stooped in a room in the forgotten part of the house. She was an only child, ignored and occasionally treasured. On whims, her mother decided to be a pushy stage type, desperate for her daughter to hit the big time in any way possible. She enrolled her in Pony Club, ballet lessons, beauty pageants and precocious debating societies. She asked Lucy for articulate opinions on current affairs at dinner. TV and processed sugars were only permitted on wet Saturdays.

On other days—from waking onwards—Lucy's mother screamed blue murder at the child. She'd rant how hard it was to keep her biggest regret alive—to watch the thing that made her piss leak breathe and grow. Lucy didn't mind too much; mother would slump in front of the TV turned up full blast during her diatribes. Worst was when there was no dinner. "I ain't feeding the fucking leech tonight until she starts earning her keep," mother shouted to a silent father in his locked study. "I don't give a monkeys about these new-fangled paper rounds. She ain't gonna be the next Pete Sampras. Who am I kidding. My mother and her mother's mother and the mother before that have all been Sheela na gigs. It's in our blood, what we're famous for. It's the family bleedin business."

With no pocket money, Lucy had to forage for nettles in the fields attached to the back of the house. With stinging skin she'd carry a hot bowl of soup upstairs and sob while it cooled down. Then she'd sip it as slowly as possible to shift focus from mum's words. She'd mouth lonely smoke signals out of the window at rabbits and a sparse cross that marked the bones of her pony. The rabbits had myxmytosis, stewing in red-eyed broods.

A blasé waiting-room agony; they've done all their crying.

The rackets and skis and Latin lessons were put aside. Lucy's induction into the family business had begun. Her hidden creasing inspired papier-mâché models that her parents inspected nightly after dinner. Sometimes there were guests: admirers and informal advisers. Often there were loiterers—twitchy mac wearers—waiting outside for autographs. Lucy's ancestors were the first mass-manufacturers of the nudie zoetrope and the family was still a minor draw for collectors.

Grown Billy—all crags, spikes and shakes—was one of them.

He stalks through backstreets, grumbling at the mug in the air, the cut of your jib, dragging his dead leg against the kerb, ear to the ground. He's on the lookout for pulses, pacemakers, wanton tickings. He carries stigmata for a third eye and a slit throat gesture made with finger. But he's a soft sort really. A quiet type. He smudges his hologram self against office workers and adult cinema exiters. He lingers when given his change, thinking of something to say. An astute observation. Weather talk. The latest planning permission. The price of tuna.

The dead summer.

He enters the cinema.

The screen is on its last legs; the sound phoned in. The scene is played out as it plays out as Lucy lurches in front and pulls her g-string to the side. Her dance is dead, crab-legged. She's lamb-pale behind a satin slip. The screen is at least house—maybe whale-sized. A whale's eye is the size of a fist, or maybe a dustbin lid. Whales have long lashes, longer than cows. Pause here and picture their coy winks across deaf seas.

•

She pretended to take questions from the back and via a live satellite link. She pretended to be a war correspondent, describing devastation in clipped vowels, giving gore sexy gravitas. Sometimes she couldn't decide what she was and just swayed, all lipsticked rictus for the partially sighted. That's the move mother taught her. A dad-directed dimmer-switch show banjaxed any lull. Men traipsed in dog shit and private rubble and passed on the stair. This was Las Vegas at the bottom of a canal; groping small talk the morning after.

That bit in Jaws when you saw the head.

Sometimes, tissues jerk like Titanic farewells. There are no proud in here, or they soon forget. Age is a thing built on forgetting—its skeleton a stumbling momentum.

I remember when there was flesh, and remember for those who do not.

But back to here—a nowhere place, a dark stairwell. It's been a while for Billy. He's been busy with things. Drinking. Getting dressed. Going back to bed. He didn't know the girl had grown.

Billy swears Lucy's legless as she glissandos up the aisle, reversing her seppuku with red nails. He christens her Snow Angel and exits on air. Grins across bridges that slice up this city. He designs the buildings he passes; everything for once is opening up for him, revealing new softness. No more mechanical stupors. No more hawked meat. Neat slits will wink with no eye on the time. He wakes early now and carefully shaves all his contours. Fondles shiny goods at stalls that spring up on Wednesdays. Under looping grey he stops and buys something for her wrist.

We walked into the chemist eyeing how they categorized the good stuff. Merrick asked to see different brands of eardrops while I vaulted over the counter with a handful of something calming. Some mother's milk for a blanched hue and a heartbeat. Drive it home with a hot tongue, daddy-o. I've tried them all; dick ain't no match for this gurning abyss.

Billy's back, early, trying to locate the most casual seat. G9—back row centre—says passing intrigue to him; a pit stop for a man of the world. The screen is a curiosity for a damp afternoon. He keeps his arms crossed. He's paid money for a private dance and is unsure whether this is a good idea. His heart stammers tiny protests. Should he cut his losses and leave at the end of the song? When it ends he approaches the stage, keeping his breath close to his chest. He hasn't brushed his teeth. He focuses on the shuddering ham behind Lucy, behind Snow Angel.

"How's your dad?" he asks, all dazed blinks.

"Fine," says Lucy, jabbing at the dark's back. Billy follows her skulking to a stale room. *Is the Duchess watching?* His mouth is at home here. There's a ghetto blaster on a table and a peeling chair, stuffing seeping from brown pleather shanks. Mouse droppings and magazines full of dated fashions. With Lucy's back turned, Billy's hands begin a flustered voguing he can't stop. *Oh Jesus let me be appropriate for once.* "For forty quid more you can have a special dance," she says as she skips through tracks—spurts of the dead and the dying on the reunion trail.

"That'd be nice," says Billy. He thinks his heart might dribble out of his trouser legs, confessing guts and forgets. Lucy's eyes roll round the houses. She turns around.

I am surviving the falls; they are bored.

Tinny honky tonk of Hank Locklin's "Geisha Girl"—a minor hit from the '50s. Lucy mimes a parasol grasp before resorting to her trusty sways. Billy counts breaths from infinity backwards. Everything here is measured. Gulped. She is near real. The numbers keep scrolling. The impact of groin on brain verges on unfair. She carries on even more uncommitted, a déjà vu in a dark room. Billy can hear his insides and wonders what it means. If his arse-sweat will leave a visible mark when he stands. Will he come like a hanged man? Would she hold it against him?

Lucy lies on the floor now, her sturdy legs wide open taunting muscle and hate. Billy's eyes spread; his heart heaves to see her honed in on. He bets in her he'll taste god and nectarines. She pretends to frig herself while moving her legs semaphorely, tracing the damp swirling on a ceiling jaundiced with convected regret. She wishes she was wearing her rollerskates, silver and blue and blurry with speed.

A PETTY DEATH

Her dad's death is neatly assuaged in a late-night murmuring era. It's not yet complete, but there are crying walks across fields, alone. He'd seen Roy Orbison once, at Caesars Palace. *Cry-i-i-i-ing over you.*

Lucy smokes and watches and thinks on the family business. The picture has bruised edges she can't touch, not even with her ring finger. The rabbits aren't moving and mum is stalling her words. They trail off in unthinking, as smoky letters across sky. Her dressing gown belt wilts to the floor. She broods in her tea-making; there's not enough milk. Pouring glides into tepid stirring, then forgetting. Where are the biscuits—did she leave them in the car? Did she buy any? It's Sunday and the shops are shut. The women sit apart while the dog concedes into a quarter circle. Deciding against life, dreaming the end. Light lays a sickly wash on grass; legs buckle on dew. Neighbours whistle while washing cars. Grey water meanders to their doors in indifferent dowsing. Lucy steps outside in her nightie. Her bare feet buoyed by wet grit. She's overstretched but can't sleep. It's too late to go back to bed. The rooms stay dazed, their shadows console but are strained, flinching from hardness and insult. They give up at night, shrinking into quiet and knowing. An impotent slinking on the landing. A passing day. A sloughing of tender pride from bone. *I told you so.* Moths move above a piss in the dark. Someone has left the room. A sloppy grin at a pale ceiling. *Lucy, let down your hair.*

She sits facing Billy while tossing spaghetti. She rubs it up and down, in circles of denial, letting it climb up walls and collapse off steel. She's not hungry nor going anywhere so morbidly waits, making murder at the table. She is aware of uncertainty as a bathing halo— her crooked chair against tile, her future, whether the waiter will swat his glance at Billy miming the bill. She eyes the odds of her rollerskating dreams versus the business of brusque labial display. She does not want to be pinned, pressed among promised hurts that fall in sequence. She sees pain as a family crest in stained glass, glinting pitfalls that confront. There's only so much inverted yearning she can take—the rest just disgusts.

"I brought you a present," says Billy, a knock-off in his sweaty clamp. He's been counting his blinks up to this moment, exalting in newer seeing and the happiness that waits for him this time. It is his for once, not made of piled dirt nor deserted on a causeway. His exiled years have ended, this is his last push into togetherness—a glossy terminal moraine. No more Guinnessed mornings waiting for the postman or being chased round tables with snapped pool cues. No more Alzheimered desire and stunned hardness. He wonders will his stools be firmer now; he won't have to hide or stoop or smudge himself, folding paper like confessions. The greatest want rests in his lap. He feels casually death-proof among the romancing and birthdaying units stacked across tile.

"Sorry?" says Lucy.

WHEN I WAS NOTHING BUT MOTION

Inside dead time my face glides in stately fugue aimless but always with testudo conviction. Attacking when cornered but never cornered rubbery prosopon ink past and rattle my footing my coordinates never known. I skate under the sound of someone bleeding on me.

Near-naked dead-end regret brought to life and pawed by eyeless packs at graffitied bus stops. This is what goes on in the suburbs after sundown. An ape chorus bends and howls guernincally at what will only get worse in comfortable footwear. Pushy parents fine-tooth the programme on the front row. Tact stands in the wings in pissy knickers knock-kneeing and mouthing missed cues. The cripples at the starting line are ready for their close-ups. The getaway car is long gone.

Dad says we need firewood for the barbecue so I skip past the rabbits to the fairy trees. I'm young and know my hands are small but the fairies are smaller still. I must be careful not to trample but my palms are the safest valleys. I can't see them but I've sewn doll furniture into the trees' branches. If I see them moving I'll know I'm not alone, that I'm safe at night, that I don't need Jesus to carry me over pavement cracks. I keep watch but nothing moves under shadow. But how will I know something is moving when I can't stay still? My knees raw from the skating tricks I try on the patio. I stall my hurt and whimper for later. I am Pearl: the prettiest in Starlight Express.

I'm pissing warmth in my hiding place, crouched and keen to be found, for touch and death and the same kind tide I felt angled in my pony's saddle. I wanted to go again but mum said it was someone else's turn. My eyes older now, warm and rolling back, stroking their harsh sockets, remembering. Too much sugar in my arteries. My mouth gapes silent prayers. How my mother helped me roll my tights up to my waist and lifted me into laughs. I was light and flat back then. Gravity caved and the good lived. Sickness was flimsy, shaken like dust from my neat body. A tight ball I could curl into. The safety I'll never feel again. The crinkled heat and dog splat in the shade, his panting salty. The flowers' scrunching joy and us pinching petals for keeps. He waits for my next move. I whisper in his ear about my ailments and he shuts his jaws. Dogs die young because they don't need to learn how to live. By the end he could not stand and all I could think was he'd drunk from the sea.

CRIPPLE CABARET

Their scraping embraces were projected and paused onto the back room's wall. They were two black boxes colliding in dark, speaking through slack string. Kitsch objects new to their cold fat and its mooning glow. Mother—a drunk's Edith Piaf—and her latest fancy man tutting and perched on pleather. Picking at chicken bones and Lucy in fleshy moments. "Your angles are all wrong," says Steve, picking fat from his teeth. "And he's blatantly flat-lining, poor old fella."

"She's always too much in here," says mum, skull-tapping with a greased yellow finger. "Skating and dreaming and not thinking about dad and England. It was the same when she was small. You should be rubbling yourself, but where are you? You can't do that if you're not there in the first place, love."

Lucy crosses her legs. "I know what I'm doing mum."

"I think sometimes you want us to go under. You enjoy my suffering. It's a cheap holiday." Her croak is barren, all business and grind. She smokes kissily right up to the butt ends, no time for kind words. "I can't stop those walks of his. It's all our land. You have to focus on now and your current contortion. Steve's doing a great job with the lights—you can almost see your organs. I've only seen more disappointment from black lungs on a fag packet. Imagine dad's eyes are the blue lights. His proud glare at your bits. You have no excuse."

Time ain't time memory never was where there's a will there's a family there is nothing truer than that people come in and out of your life your wife family once and not for the first time the usual fuckers in droves whose faces bleed into everything else well-wishers squatting past politeness the door shown not a budge no courtesy leeching our last moments our lost ones meant for just us the Duchess and me not a hint taken waves and waves of bad breeding no manners the fuckers endless visits she didn't want your cheering-up stories and hectic schedules your children's afterschool activities condolences you fuckers she's weren't gone yet sympathy cards with the price still on the back bygones eh what do they mean by bygones when her smell still hangs heavy in the room fortified wine and four cans and the job nicely done you're not a drunk if you don't get drunk and the paper gone up in price what's a few pence when there's coins stuck on the window sill treasure down sofa sticky greenish the Latin fading life ain't bad at times Snow Angel likes me some days her rosebuds in blue light seen her smiling when she doesn't think I'm looking it's not about draining me there's no malicious method the little I have my reasons and upsets no one's business but mine and Her upstairs an attractive older man an urban silver fox ready for living and loving again but if I'm honest if I'm truthful I'll almost tell the truth but not now eh no siree and you darling you keep shtum upstairs not pretending Angel doesn't notice the leg but we're all flaws I'm still human at heart still loveable that'll be Graham—

Billy rubs crumbs from trousers and toes threadbare slippers. It's an effort to get up, to shake from deep thought that can occupy him til *Wheel of Fortune* in the afternoon ... at the earliest. Sometimes he finds himself the following morning unsure whether he's slept, where he might have been in the night, rumination a damn continent on his trousers.

Final reminders collapse onto the mat before he can get to the door. He opens it and calls out, stopping the postman's escape. "Many parcels today?" *Say something interesting for once you eejit.*

"Not too bad today, Billy. Not too bad. How you been keeping? Thought you were on holiday, haven't seen you down the pub."

"Not flush enough for that at the moment," says Billy, scratching itchless skin and inspecting the sunburn on Graham's nose. *How will I speak to two heads if I start seeing double what's polite and which one will I address first start from the outside in never did learn how to debone a fish swallow everything with a smile and a thank you.* He enjoys his chats with Graham—the booze's smoothness is at its optimum smothering with awkwardness a dormant assassin.

"Oh I know how that is," says Graham, patting skeletal strands. "Missus takes the piss these days."

Billy beams a "don't I know it," no longer a cack-handed boomerang into quiet. His cul-de-sac crags lift into glad knowing he wants seen. "Women, eh."

"So there's a woman in the picture now then? You sly old dog. Local bird?"

"Nah," says Billy.

"Not one of the students across the way is it? They were sunbathing out the front yesterday. Cracking girls. Tops off. Very tidy."

"Even better. Not from around here. A classy type."

Graham's eyes scan over a stained T-shirt, a defunct software firm freebie. "Ooh, a mystery woman is it? Just as well you're splashing the cash on her and not down the pub Billy. Mad Sinbad was in the other night ... asking after you."

THE WARMTH AND UNSAID IN THE CAR

He sees himself as he was once: helpless, the youngest, all bundled knees as wheels underneath churn soil. A cramped dirge across barrenness in a Vauxhall hatchback, all child-locks and muted morning breath. The driver's hand a benign clamp on gearstick, his gold ring glinting. His Pampas grass eyebrow in rearview mirror and eye locked on the cloying now. Sand-headed men smother their yawns. Pigeons pick bones in the cold. Billy wants to say something, to call it off with a ghost-limbed group hug. His belly rumbles into rain-pocked sides of dampness seeping out over a baby-seat. A hint of piss and a bloating inevitability. A photo of the Duchess. Her mute, snowy face in his wallet spoons the queen's. She says nothing and reveals less. Weighty, tired squints imbricate on the rubbish outside, mixing with gulls and spoils. "The cattle are lowing, Billy. The buck stopped a while back." Sinbad turns the radio down. Billy can still hear the Shipping Forecast. The *there there*'s of Cromarty and Dogger. The waves knocking against a little boat lost on the North Sea. To be a man of lulls and escapes and a radio career. Matching monographed his 'n' hers slippers placed the right way under the bed. A full stomach and kind waking to days spread like a picnic blanket. Careful folding and a hand held in the hospital. Quiet structure shared. Tears grace-noted, smoothed with soft fingers. The gentleness brought to dying skin. *I looked at her with big slabs of eye, big ol' china plates, I was drinking her in as I knew it'd be the last time. Us sinking ships together, toe-dippers at the brink. Me losing my footing, a trip over a rabbit hole, hobbling agony of my heart stopping on a missed stair.* It's all too late, his was never the right horse, he's a last-minute Houdini understudy against a slow clapping tide.

"I never understood a word he ever said—it was just sausage meat snipped with intakes of breath. It was years before I realized he was using words."

•

"Not dad," the mother says.

"No rabbits?" the daughter says.

"None."

"Oh."

"Steve. The cinema. Says he's above this now."

"Where?"

"Fringe theatre."

"Never."

"I said he could kick in the back doors."

"Mum."

"He still turns away."

"What now."

"Gameshows eventually. When they're about to lose everything."

"Our fields."

"High-rise."

DOWSER AT A BUSH FIRE (daddy)

Far too conscious Billy too tender by half breathes relentlessly, mulling it over. His fly open as he lingers at lights, biting dead skin off his lips as bad news. He crosses roads without clocking cars, courting impact, wanting more than broken bones. Across sleepless hours he cannot bring himself to name the man— the sailor—or see his face—just as cliff-faced as his. He squints a TV noise mask and gets up to make tea whenever it sings (the voice muscles barks on a bad line). What can the sailor want? How'd he get back? They'd parted on rough seas with Mad Sinbad ending up shipwrecked in Malaga. He was last seen on TV news cowering naked in a panic room behind a knock-off Green Lady painting, then—after the ad break—wrapped in a towel for an interview. Billy kept the newspaper cuttings in a box under his bed. It was soon forgotten about, besides the odd vacuum bump in anticipation of a female body bathed by a blue moon.

Another long night of libations and otiose lines drawn on paper. *The gaps will put a stop to all this madness that's where I'll find sleep in warmth as soft as girl's skin.* It's the milky whiskey that does the trick finally, cradling Billy with a kick. Later he wakes in his damp armchair and stands and groans at the heavy day, the sky's belly bulging over him. What's its promise this time—will it be different for once? No. That's not how it works. Hell seeps through holes in shoes. He feels unsteady, no Muybridge assurance propels him. He takes the long way round avoiding stairs and escalators—he doesn't trust his feet nor their edges. In loose loops he surrounds the cinema—he knows Snow Angel is the only one who can sort this mess. He's ashamed. Too old for all this. But the sad girl on top of the tree is put there for a reason. *She'll surely laugh.* He veers into the back alley that brings him close. Bouncers nod as Billy passes. He's convinced cracks in the pavement will pull him through.

He sways in sweats, trying to soften his pants as he knocks and waits and grips onto silence, the siphoned good bits. *You're a man of the world Billy these shakes aren't you just your snake skin that you ain't cleaned up yet. You need to get your house in order pal. You forget. Women aren't keen on stink and mess.* The door opens on a tight chain, the sparrow madam flexing a kohled eye at the alley. Billy sees a child til he spots her sour mouth. A pale-lightning wonder if she ever danced ... could she still take a dick? "What is it?" she yawns at his tired shoes. His tongue lolls in darkness. "We're not open," says the little sparrow, shutting the door. Billy butts in: "I need to see Snow—Lucy. Please." "You can't see her cos we've closed. No more dances. Finished. Maybe a commemorative zoetrope in the future if we get Chinese backing."

"Billy," says another voice from an open window above. Billy gazes up at Lucy's curls rippling in the bin breeze. He swallows stiffly. "It's alright mum. He can come in."

Hell is a thing that happens to you … you could be happening anywhere.

See Billy against hard slants, gasping upwards in desperate gestures. He's pulling teeth with his teeth: messy business. His sweats and shakes break their banks. But the sparrow gave the nod—"just this once without payment,"—and his blood tries to recall its useful directions. His bad leg revenges each stagger, but he won't let it stop him getting to Lucy's room. This is his chance. She'll sit on the tip of his tongue, bleeding the bad past and rubble. He can't wait for the blissed, moaned tipping before his death in consummation, his shuddered ache and bolted brain dripping in soft arms. *Oh let it rain down Angel, my grey matter puddling at your pretty feet. I bet they're small and perfectly formed. They're right to call it a little death; what's past is done with.*

She sits in front of a missing-bulbed mirror, corpse washing, powdering her tantrumy eye gently. Shiny oddments from blackmail scatter the room and the skin beneath her neck with a delicate name. Smoke and dust jitter about her in a spooked squall. Half her face is clean, empty, a Dora Marr shard not in on the joke. She's kind but firm with her eye—this is not a place for skirting or niceties. "Angel what happened?" says Billy, overcast.

"Oh, nothing. The usual. New landlord's a bit hands on." Lucy reaches for eye-shadow, a missing shade of blue. Billy's hands move onto her shoulders from nowhere, pawing fossils without evolution. Lucy sighs and looks up for the first time. "And we're fucked for lights—Steve's done a runner. We're back to the dimmer switch and torches. Mum's got arthritis in her fingers so can't do it fast enough." Lucy demonstrates with a lighter. "She was making me dance to R&B. Moving with the times she said, embracing modern romance. The lyrics—if you could hear them! No heart, Billy. They could tell mine wasn't in it. No sad pulse, not a clue to one. I only like Country music. It has to be Country. Dad loves Country." She gets up, lights a cigarette and shuts the window. "We're saving money being closed. Mum's trying to work things out but she can't make sense of Dad's books. It's all hieroglyphics to us."

"Yeah, numbers are tricky."

"Nah, it's actual hieroglyphics, Billy. Dad's a clever man. Lightning quick. He doesn't need a calculator. Very private too—we're not allowed in his study. We went down the British Museum and had a look at the Rosetta stone, but no luck. Mum got in trouble with a security guard … she only wanted a closer look—she'd forgot her glasses." Lucy hands Billy a scrapbook filled with the cinema's crayoned secrets.

"Where's your dad now?"

"He said he was going dowsing. He's a big deal in the industry … or was. The Elvis of dowsing they called him. It was a minor craze for a while—everyone going at it with bent coathangers. There was even a novelty single—"Dowsing Dude." It just missed the Top 40. And a line dance to go with it. It was a magical time. But then the drought of '98 happened. The hosepipe ban. First it was a few dried-up hanging baskets, then peoples' koi carp got hit. Garden ponds full of death. British summer time ruined. At first they blamed the EU. Then they started blaming dad, said he was a con artist, or that he'd siphoned it all off somewhere. Like he had a secret reservoir or something! People went mad with the coathangers, but no one could find a drop. We thought it'd pass … it was ridiculous really. Silly season. Then a bloke in Norwich got one through the neck … that's when it changed. It was nothing to do with dad, but you can imagine … it didn't make me popular at school I can tell you. It's calmed down now of course, but you can still clear a room with dowsing talk. It crushed him. He'd hyperventilate a lot in the supermarket. At traffic lights. On the phone. And then the hieroglyphics started. When he's not doing the cinema he'll be in his study. He says he likes hieroglyphics cos vowels have no meaning … whatever that means. But he still likes to practice his craft in secret. You can lose it you see—your dowsing sensibility. You have to keep it warm, 'keep the old taps running' dad says. It can freeze over if you're not careful … then you're fucked. He checks our land against maps, that it's not getting smaller. He says you can't trust maps. They scar what's clean. Mum says he's gone for good. She's a liar though, a jealous old thing. She's not as smart as dad. I think the truth is in there. He's written where he is and he's waiting for me to come find him. He wants rid of her. He's sick of the business. Wants a new start. He wants to be a scholar and me to be dancer. He can't say that though obviously. She's run this business into the ground. You know it's bad when the disabled have fucked off. I could be in musicals Billy ... I don't give a shit about all this." Lucy's sobs stun them both. Billy stays where he is, an old fool in a dirty mirror.

The weak fizz of last night's lemonade on my bedside table and mum shouting I'll be late. I always wake before I trip into a rabbit hole, but sometimes I look down and my ankles feel ready to snap in sunless fields, beyond ours. Near where they dredged a pond for a missing man and our hedge was on the news. I never hunted for tadpoles after that. I told no one at school.

I am silver and blue and blonde, a beautiful flag. I bask in my tricks. I make flamenco dancers look like clock-watchers. I know the judges won't see this, that they can't weigh what I carry. They don't see the wounded bird in my hands. They'll focus on my voice and feet, my budding, my pretty nose. I'll skate better than all of them; I'll be Pearl. I'll bite chunks out of the vague. I'll brain any bitch. Mum combs my hair before I gulp and go in.

My breathing is ahead of me, small-talking to the future.

BRANDING OUR FORGETTING (never odd or even)

"Weeping Lipizanners rearing up into fat hearts ... chicken in a basket ... stuffing breast and thighs ... no brown meat ... oriental surprise ... desserts on fire ... stunt girl splits ... sparklers for the stiffest ... classy like Crazy Horse ... Paris ... *dix points* from the French judge ... crying girl cabaret ... the erotica of women providing for their futures ... blue jokes and money notes ... Mona Lisa money shot ... Lucy in a cage ... little bird with a sad song ... daddy daddy please come here ... Marilyn mouthing 'help' at JFK ... sewed in but not for long ... billboard up to the guts ... neon slits at slowing cars ... cross-sections of anatomical desire ... Hawaiian-themed evenings ... lager in coconuts ... loose ladies nights ... scarf dance to *Lady In Red* ... tassels on rosebuds ... iced nipples out back ... wanking with feeling ... mood lighting ... lava lamps ... vulgar vegetable competitions ... lasers for exotic gymnastics ... shoe-shine service ... disabled access ..." Billy stops his pitch with sweat heavy on his back like bone.

Lucy and the sparrow listen. With the cinema shut there's nothing else to do, no buckets and spunky mops to wrangle. "What makes him so sure about all this," says the sparrow, her cracks ganging up in softer parts. "What's his story in this business besides his rod?"

Billy looks at Lucy who sits shivering, grinding empty circles with gum. He remembers the old Abcat adult cinema on Cally Road, how his gait changed after the first time. Bending down to tie his lace outside, still in two minds, the tight looping goading him, hinting at promise in the dark. He paid the entrance fee with warm coins. Inside he could not spread his eyes wide enough. The full bushes' blown-up and blatant luxuriousness. The slobbered muck, a spider's web in winter cemetery light. The sheer industrious joy of pistons and hams unrelenting. His rattling hurt caved again and again. Clocking regulars on his row, dropping off with the end of a lunch break, a building's completion or just old age. Basic scenarios, badly fitted costume dramas badly dubbed. With heart though, for family men and the modern gent.

And sometimes—just sometimes—a girl on screen might remind him how it was with the Duchess, when she was alive.

That's what Billy tried to remember as he stood outside, dazed among the debris. Steam rose from his burnt hands while a dropped cigarette destroyed the cinema's seats and most of the men on them. The exits had been satisfactory, the police said. The fire's glare was an angry wall spitting flames onto pavement. The screen melted to stamp-size—a lonely box of continental flesh returning its gaze at long last. It silently watched the male throng failing to scramble onto a single turntable ladder. Those left inside were given neat obituaries, clipped nods and a sparse spread well within the clock. There was neither loitering nor appetite, no coats removed. Their end and its place would always jar, taking the place of divorcees, cancer and other deathly taboos. They became unknown men, or muffled mentions in hurried passing, foreign names no one knew how to pronounce. For the older ones, the drifters and the determinedly separated, their uncollected ashes may as well have been left on the tube, circling until the trains go to sleep ... wherever that is.

Billy stays mute while Lucy smacks gum. He knows this is his last chance—all those other ones were frauds, tests ... this one's the real deal. "I've had plenty of success in my life," he starts, as measured as haiku, his semi settling. "I was in computers for a long time. Dot com dial up you name it ... you know about computers yeah? The Internet? Like when you buy a book online—ever do that Lucy? And it comes up with the 'people who bought this book also bought' recommendation? Well, I invented that. It came to me in a dream. Some people in computers say it was as important a development as the wheel ... I've always been an innovator y'see. I'm always coming up with new ideas, new ways of seeing old things. I'm too fast for evolution. Evolution's there blinking hard wondering where I went haha ... I adjust fast to the climate. I'll grow gills if I have to. I can turn anything into opportunity. You know when you wake in the morning and the ceiling is the floor and you think am I really stuck up here with all the clutter? Why can't I be down there in all that space? Why can't I get down from here? I'm not supposed to be up here. I'm better off down there. But I've got to stay up here for the time being. Fine by me, I'll thrive in the clutter ... of course everyone thinks it's an Amazon thing now, but I was there first. The little guy is always bumped off history."

Lucy lifts a drawn-on brow, as exact and dwelled upon as its neighbour. "What use is that to us," says the sparrow with ventriloquist finesse.

Lucy's mother softened after several hours of bar charts, graphs and pies scrawled and stuck to the walls with gum. Billy's laser pen—pointing at peaks and profit margins on the backs of unpaid bills—convinced her of a future for the cinema, a potential global empire for the family brand.

Billy explained that Lucy would be the star attraction of the new cinema, the jewel in the belt buckle of the lonesome ladies man. She'd be perfect and brutalized, no shaving bumps or glaze of drugged endurance in sight. He reckoned that stray day-tripper dads could be reeled from their dry wives and kept in the cinema's seats by raunch and rollerskating skill. Lucy was a stifled star, he said, with only a pinhole to shine through. She needed a grand stage, flattering lighting and a supporting cast of barely legals, runaways and foreign medical students. Maybe even the theatre crowd—dismayed at the queues and ticket prices for Les Mis—could be enticed through the back-alley doors. The girl deserved to be seen he said, her come-to-bed eyes on a billboard with the whole city disgusted and spunking as one. Headachey wives would find her on their husbands' phones, booted and pouting. There'd be spin-off lines, a touring show, a renaissance in skating that hadn't been seen since the '90s inline craze. And no Amazon at the end swallowing them up—the family empire would stay theirs.

The women were blank by this point, tired from talk of bottom and chorus lines. "But what will dad think about all this?" asked Lucy.

"He'll be proud," said Billy.

The sparrow sat forward. "This is what he wanted for you all along, love. What we both wanted. The secondary sex characteristics meant nothing. How about a few Country numbers, eh Billy. Wouldn't that go down well? A few torch songs for daddy."

'80s lukewarm saxophone oozes around a white-suited man on a stepladder, tipping food into a panoramic fish tank. These are flimsy movements from a man built to bulldoze, his bare head quarried to get the job done. His shadow a timid animal compared to the tank's bubbles of forgetting, their hurried insistence on escape. Candelabra light lilts on his forehead sweat forming a bland compress. He is too warm, overdressed, and the room has too much carpet and fur to not be a hibernation chamber. A Maltese dog—a white bit of a thing—laps at its balls on a stiletto-shaped chair, a blind stab at interior sophistication. The dog is never walked nor looked at directly—its matted reign on the leopard-print shoe is treated with a reverence so deep its function has been waylaid.

On the walls are framed pictures of Mad Sinbad, the bouldered man with a boxer's nose still balancing mid-feed. He grins the same paving slabs across the row of spot-lit photos, his pally death-grip on minor celebrities, all confused, cross-eyed, staking mild crisis vividly. There are newspaper clippings of run-ins and melting time, his quotes highlighted and asterisked. "I maintain it was self-defence," he says in most of them. "But yeah, I'm taking anger management classes."

Sinbad had been an outspoken campaigner against daylight saving, not changing the clocks in his pubs and clubs in winter while the rest of the British Isles retreated into the archaic custom. More leisure time was the future, he said. Man had a right to more wine, women and song. The swaggering hour gave him an invincible sheen, respectability and a blink-and-you'll-miss-it cameo on a TV soap opera. He was a hit. The sailor had finally arrived.

Surgical storms localized and jaws dripping the devil leapt up in a red room the fur made him soundproof I never throw anyone out tie them up and put them down in the bloody boiler house til I'm ready for em

It hadn't all been glory in blunt gestures—bad choices often left him moorless. His roving empire—dented and hungrier after the Abcat gutting—found itself backed into more dead-ends and kicked-in back doors. His pals at the council could ignore his sloppy flails for only so long. He'd stopped trying with his drug fronts, too busy chasing auditions for minor gangster roles in straight-to-video films. Too busy staring into a ladies compact at Hollywood veneers gone wrong, he'd failed to notice his cannabis farmers whitewashing a shop unit every day until dark to mask the tell-tale scent of its insides. The two men—who felt they'd come up in the world from flogging straight-to-video DVDs in supermarket carparks—spent hours every day painting and re-painting the shop's exterior, finishing one coat only to start another. Neighbours remembered them as friendly but quiet types who—although they did not appear to be professional painter-decorators—

were dogged in repetition. "We wondered what was going on," remembered one local curtain twitcher. "They weren't wearing overalls and their brushes were a bit on the small side." The paint was still drying during the shop's raid, the painters too knackered to protest. Sinbad was long gone on a boat headed for Spain. He stayed there in boozy exile, holding court and practicing his darts stance in British-themed pubs. The long grip of the law finally dragged him back to a cell and occasional exercise under drizzle. Recently released and unfazed, Sinbad decided that things would be different this time. Less razzmatazz—less softly softly—his gob's slabs would not shy from blood's hard stain. He was determined to be all business, to crack skulls when needed. He'd already made a league table; poor old Billy wasn't far from the top.

NEWFANGLED UNCONSOLER

It's me, mother; muffled and crotchless. I'm on the other end of the line. The bad side, past the slack. Cornered in a pissy tardis, breathing through my mouth, trying not to step outside of lines luminous with someone's stink.

The walls reveal the girlfriend experience is never counted in sequence. The cars roar and I will not go on. I tire of visions of tanned pistons. I hobble headless outside, bawling from concrete lack. Mother, are you still there?

Mean rain beats hard on me. Blood cells swerve on a neon grid. I scatter myself across slick streets, dodging ferocious force and matter, shouting regret at metal. My anger grows surface. I am shoeless; muddy-eyed with grudge.

I walk into a chain restaurant and sit facing a shrinking woman who gave me lovely teeth. Those neat slabs designed for precise first kisses with older boys—where are they now? She knows I'm here. Her poise is empty, propped up. The ethered silence spreads between us while we wait for our starters.

"What could you see."

"Not a breeze."

"Dad?"

"A saint's patience."

"Where is he."

"Playing blind."

What did mother know? At the washing line shrouded by willows more times than there was washing. What was she really doing back there? Was she alone?

Life is elsewhere; I know my distance.

"Why in the dark."

"Afraid to think."

"Who was there?"

There were no straight answers. Mum came back wet at dusk on dry days. She sighed as she traipsed her squelching boots upstairs. Lucy could not understand where the damp came from—it was hosepipe ban season, the first since '98. Mother's entrances were followed by showers with clothes on, beer knocked back hard under the gush. Lucy watched, sitting on the bog, holding a dry towel. "Please," she bleated into the bathroom mist. She wished for anything, not just dad and desiccation. The house had started to bleed. Ceilings bulged with running water. There was so much to rescue in the damp, even what was dead. She was not sure about herself in all of this, where it was safe to stand in a condemned building. She tried her best—mopping up mum's incessant slop, trimming mushrooms that started to peek through the moistness.

Then fire became a concern. Mum lay in bed after her showers, smoking a cigarette bouquet and ashing her pale chest. Lucy stole fire extinguishers from public libraries, dragging them up the stairs to surround the bed. When not passing out with a burning bush in her mouth, mum threw each new arrival out the window. The neighbours invited friends over to watch Lucy's struggle lifting them back inside. Each sob and metal knock against stair was met by tuts and wide-eyes behind thin walls, more meat on the barbeque. Under her blushes and garden fence small-talk, Lucy convinced herself that the Sisyphean ordeal meant she was loved and loving without end, that it had goaded her stamina and dancer's litheness into new being.

Fried onions and local ale good to myself bank account in the dog's name they never thought of that eh investors more like protestors every one of my good ideas the fuckers dogs given human names it's not right always the woman the egg not up to the job woman a round shape not enough conviction for edges they're all talk all soft blame always someone else's fault a man's multitasking can't sit still eggs a poached one the healthiest kind fifty sit-ups today by lunch would my son age like me just as well there's none but women don't tell you their one silent subject a dynasty across continents a rainbow family lines in my cheeks getting worse scrubbing won't shift maybe I'll start a flattering head-tilt like Princess Di did she do that in the last photo slumped in the back bet she did vain cow Liverpool Care Pathway in the news again poor dying sods having to drink water out of flower vases the will to live a terrible thing really Liverpudlians' victim complex any excuse to tie a teddy bear to a railing public outpouring of grief but who cleans the rotting flowers up at the end and those cards with the price tag still on the back does she see a silver fox I know she doesn't fake it anymore that'll be Graham with the girdle—

Billy beats the postman to the door for once, crease-free and crumbless in waiting. He's eager to share his recent success, to banter as an equal, to test his new cinched silhouette. He calls after the man, who's already retreated after dumping the package against Billy's door. "Sorry mate, can't stop," says Graham, more eyes-down than usual. He spills his letters onto the floor (mostly final notices and postcards from suicidal seaside resorts waiting to fall into the ocean). Billy goes to help. "It's fine, I've got it."

"No mate, let me," says Billy. Two men bend in a strange altar ritual. "Why don't you come in for a drink Graham, we haven't had a good chat in a while. I've got so much to tell you. New woman news, a new business venture, could be something in it for you pal. And it's not like the computers—there's no risk. Safe as houses. Money-back guarantee— guaranteed. I really mean it this time." A light hand on Graham's shoulder. There is something else here with them, something eyed, a cloaked jitteriness.

"Thanks for the offer mate but I'm flat-out. Gotta go."

"Aw, come on now. What's the rush?"

"Get to fuck! Get away." The postman's brown teeth chomp bitter air. "It's always you Billy boy isn't it. Always looking to shaft someone, even when backed in a stinking corner. It was the future you said. Mine and Jeff's. Surefire success you said. Retirement and a place in the sun. Poor old Jeff eh. It was the shame that did him in. The utter shame. But I'm never rude am I. Never tell you what I think. Never dump your mail in a ditch ... but it's all final notices isn't it Billy. I can tell by the font. Forgive and forget the missus said. Win some lose some. You're a sad lonely man she said. You've had a tough life. We should feel sorry for you. The twins are off to university now. Not once did you ask after them. All these years. You still stuck in this stinking piss-hole. He's back now, I told you. I said I hadn't seen you. You'd gone up north, moved away got cancer or something. Said I wasn't sure. People fade out of life. You can never really tell if they're coming or going til the death notice in the paper. Didn't have to do that did I, covering your arse. He's in every night now. Sits at the bar. I can't pot a ball with him watching. He stands next to me in the bog. Pissed all over my shoes. Said is there a problem Graham. Said I seemed awfully nervous. Said the twins look very mature now. Says he wants a chat with you. None of this is to do with me. It's over Billy. For a long time. Look around."

Thick guilt forced me into a day job. I fondled the interview questions for too long past answers so was surprised to be there on my first day, learning about the tea-making facilities and fire exits. I made mum promise on a limit of wetness, a lag between extinguisher falls. We needed fast cash. She said something I couldn't hear behind the blazing bouquet. It might have been choking but that was always her face. Billy did his best. He arranged a meeting with a bank manager, describing himself as an adult visual co-ordinator. Sitting in our kitchen after, his stiff shirt I'd ironed now corpsed, atrocious. "He thought I was working with the blind, the daft bugger. I told him we sometimes had disabled clientele but he wasn't having any of it." Bitter spit and his mug of tea gripped to coldness. Our own lukewarm ruminations at home in the dank. Swearing of the kind we hadn't heard before. We didn't blame him. Mum's own damp slid down the walls behind. I had to step up. My dream could still be prodded down a plank, vivid and alive, crawling at all times. Billy said it wouldn't be for long.

It was data entry work, a casual place. I was on the early half-seven shift, the only woman on the team. We hunched with hoods up gulping coffee. There was no learning curve, or we were the cardboard city under it. In our morning and booze breath we were already obsolete; Indians and machines could do our work on the cheap. We were a doomed battalion taking broken weapons off our dead.

I could show my guts to the world but there I was shy. I spoke in a fidgety, chiselled voice. I daydreamed slick worlds made for skating and the steps in new routines. I collapsed words to my male boss and blushed at guessed stares. Running Man's was the worst.

He sat at the corner desk, close-shaved and suited at all times. He never took off his sunglasses. He jogged around the office and stretched leisurely at the vending machine. I had to wait nearby studying staff notices and the Heimlich manoeuvre with coins warming my palm. I presumed his name derived from his businessy hurry or referenced a sporting aside to our graft's sarcastic typing. His always sounded like boasts, or bitty *I-told-you-sos* getting angrier as the hours marched.

Running Man kept his sunglasses on all winter even as more darkness slumped on already dark days. I imagined underneath was a single bloody weeping crater. If anyone was unloveable it was him, I'd decide on Monday mornings. I'd stare when I felt sure he wasn't looking. Underneath was what unlovable looked like—the sea where it began.

A wedding ring was found in a men's toilet cubicle one mid-week afternoon. No one claimed it. It was the talk of our team in that it provoked sounds from our mouths that weren't grunts. The owner had been having a sly wank we reckoned after five minutes sleuthing, our first and last team building exercise. Running Man was prime suspect—his shades were clearly for the discrete collection of wank bank material. I could understand this; our line of work—its mute monotony—lent itself to desperate scrabbles for relief. Colleagues would turn up gakked-up, unable to see straight or log on to their machines. Bumps were snorted for elevenses - for normalizing purposes. The gurning was cinematic but the management ignored it. We were all contenders here, trying to unpick our parts from time's flattening machine.

Nah it's not to do with him jogging around the office. Not at all. But I spose he does that to remind us who he is. The distance he covered. What he done. Or thinks he done I should say. He took a lot of time off, said he was going on an expedition. Said it was up there with Everest. Gagarin in space. Space monkey more like, we said. But he came back all suntanned and said he'd got the world record for running around the world. First man to do it. You can look it up. It was all over the news. He's got gold embossed business cards that say it. We stack them under crooked desks when he's not about. But did he do it, Lucy? They took his word and looked at a few receipts. Curry at the Taj Mahal. Bubble bath at the Great Barrier Reef. War zone sprints. Record breaker my arse. Record breaking fantasist, more like. So desperate to be something. Wasn't where he said he was half the time. Not even close. He was down the pub when he was meant to be dodging bullets. Someone like that doesn't have a shadow.

I'm happy staying where I am, me. I've had the same telephone number 25 years.

We were motley and tetchy but our dreaming was indivisible. We were failed and hoping and unfit for much else. Pain planned hard in all our heads. I kept my own striving secret, my face bare. I was mostly ignored. Dave, at the next terminal, was kindest. He didn't hammer his humiliation into mine. A chatty sort who'd let me in on Running Man's etymology. He was a former punk drummer deaf in one ear. Still bitter that Strummer left The 101ers. Still sad the millennium ever happened. He'd nudge me when my head hit the keyboard, then would carry on with his centripetal history of the scene's bit-part players. I was sucked into the monologue, though I had no interest in his stories of gig riots and line-up betrayals—I only cared for dad's Country songs and Starlight Express. But I loved hearing about the scene's women, severe in their alienness, their raccoon eyes and pouring flesh and insistence on now or its pushy whereabouts. I was petty compared to their youth and violent want, their cutthroat smiles. I had no hammy symbols at hand. To me the present would always be an electrified fence I took the long way around. "And the birds!" he'd remind me and I'd jolt alive. On quiet days he'd email me photos of them, their swastikas flickering under the office's etiolated light and creeping germ count. Sometimes it felt odd—why was he showing me this? Was it some kind of life coaching? A come-on? Dave wasn't like Billy. I often smelt bitterness and boozed breath but there was no hardness talking, or pining softness that

I'd hesitate to share a bed with. He said he had a daughter my age he did not see. He mentioned her when he was most glassy. He asked about my life outside work—was I studying, did I have hobbies. What did I really want to be and where did I see myself in five years. I felt sad framing answers in a pause I'd never break. I kept giggling, or forgetting to put sugar in his tea. I asked to see more photos. He sent me the one he was most proud of—a famous line-up shot of the Bromley Contingent, the most notorious and suburban punk rabble. "That's me on the end," he said, but the half skull and hunk of shoulder could've been anyone's. I felt clammy, pumped full of water, ready to burst.

•

Brando's glove-toying method orchestration girl wanting to vom contain yourself breathe lungfuls of the good stuff our scene a school gymnasium some kid's inside-out sock wedged behind apparatus proud parents and our heroine making mechanical tortured force noh expression when the wind changes back when you resort to making your mind up at long last in the school gymnasium you're a lukewarm ghost honey on shining wheels you spat and rubbed clean you're wearing a white holed sheet with an afro wig on top—askew—the competition did not require costume you made mum make one got your wires crossed in the bomb disposal that buried us you made things worse it was the best she could do in the car on the way cursing your birth forward-limbed travelling hard free dance they call it artistic expression your scores are high eighty-one seventy-eight seventy-nine eighty-three seventy-nine

•

"Can we leave now please. While he's still at the bar."

"Marion, he's buying us drinks. And he'll see us. It'll be awkward."

"I don't care now. I just wanted a quiet evening."

"I know, dear."

"I told you I didn't want to go to a British pub. Can't you say we're going back to the hotel—that you've left the trouser press on."

"No one uses the trouser press in hotels Marion ... I'm sure he'll leave us alone soon."

"Nigel, please! Just tell him I'm having a hot flush—"

"Shhh. You're the one who invited him to sit down."

"I only said there was no one sitting there."

"You *did* smile though."

"I was just being polite—it wasn't an invitation. I'm meant to be on holiday. He keeps spitting on my face. He knows he's doing it ... I'm going back to read now so give me the key."

"Alright Marge! Where you going? At least you're smiling doll."

"Oh nowhere, just to the ladies!"

"Don't be too long ... karaoke's on in a bit. Elton John and Kiki Di eh? You and me. He's been in the club, don't mind him being a poof. Nice fella, fond of the ol sniff sniff. So as I was saying Nige it was all a set up. They were out to humiliate me. Jealous of my success. I was a lone wolf not in with any cunt and they couldn't understand that."

"I see ..."

"It's like you and your landscape gardening. Let's say all the other gardeners do the same old shapes, circles and that, Calamity Brown, playing it safe. No surprises. Fair enough, not getting decapitated with the ol chain-saw, but not big dreamers y'know? Not thinking big. Not thinking of the future. And then say you're a maverick, doing errrrr ... you know, fancy stuff. Stuff that makes people slow down and have a long look. Families go on Sunday drives and all that— it's a day out to see your work. It's a soothing sight, stops the wife's headache and the kids' rows in the back seat. Well you're gonna be dismissed by the industry for a while aren't ya? Other gardeners will call you a crackpot, that sort of thing. It's cos they don't understand. They don't have the brains."

"I suppose ..."

"But you're ambitious Nige, you're thinking outside the box. And cos you're doing that and working hard at it you do well. It's Darwin, innit. You make a killing. Your gardens look pristine, cutting edge. They get jealous of you, the posh customers, the good life, the tidy missus. You're polluted with money. They haven't got the know-how to do it themselves so they want what you've got, and they can only get that by stealing it. Or trying to."

"Well gardening is very different to the nightlife industry I imagine err Sin—"

"Sinbad pal. It's alllllllllll the bloody saaaaaaaaame. We are the success stories mate. You and Marge and me—"

"It's Marion."

"Lovely looking she is, just lovely. Like a little antique doll. You ain't touched your drink Nige. You did want lager, yeah?"

"Oh yes yes, I'm just a slow drinker. I'm quite tired as well so I think we might head back."

"Well drink up my man. You'll be telling everyone back in Blighty about your night with Sinbad. Best night of the holiday! Might take em a while but then they'll twig ... 'oh, that geezer!' The flashy git who messed with time. Even Einstein couldn't manage that. That was his thing right? Or Moses. I forget. Can do a few autographs if ya like. I'm here all night."

"Oh, thank you but I think we're ok."

"I've got it—it was the little fella on wheels with the vocoder."

"Sorry?"

"I miss England a lot y'know. More than I ever thought ... the country needs men like me. We keep that little island afloat. Scotland and Wales can get to fuck though. No time for leeches, me. If I can't go back I seriously think I'll top myself. But back to the gardening story. Analogy? Is that the right word? It's French, innit. The romantic language. Easy to speak if you've just come out the dentist and the anaesthetic ain't worn off yet. Ha! Mouth full of sour marshmallows. I'm a poet, me. Always thinking in colour. I can remember the taste of every bird I've kissed downstairs. Anyway, say you done a big load of shapes Nige, hedges like proud poodles for an important customer, let's say some distant royals, yeah. Horsey looking but the wife is a piece alright. Use your imagination. *Ooh la la*. This lot are *well* bred. Even you and Margey baby are a bit of rough compared to these. And it's a nice job, she's bringing you out homemade lemonade and shortbread, you're making her laugh, having a little flirt. Nothing to worry Marge though, all strictly business. Anyway you've done a wonderful job. They'll be pleased as punch. You're a proud man. There's a polo invite with your name on it. And then in the night someone's cut their heads off, taken a chainsaw to em."

"The royals?"

"Nah Nige, the poodles! The big fack off hedge dogs you done. Ruined the facking lot. And the royals ain't happy. No stiff upper lip in sight, all wibble wibble *this is un-sat-is-fac-tory*. They could have you put in the tower for this Nige. What you gonna do about it?"

"Well, I'd urge them to contact the police ..."

"Nah, the police ain't gonna do nothing Nige. Take them out of the equation. You're a smart man. They'd stitch you up. It's up to you to sort it out."

"Well errrr ok ... perhaps i'd ask neighbours if they'd seen anyone acting suspiciously ... get the Neighbourhood Watch involved ... I'm not really sure ..."

"Nah! You know who dunnit. You facking know alright."

"I do? Oh, ok, errr... give them a call? Marion's been quite a long time, I might go check on her."

"The old gal's fine Nige. Now what you gonna do about it? Man to man."

"I'm presuming I don't have any evidence, do I?"

"You don't need it. You're a fair man. You've been made to look bad in front of royalty. This was your one chance—you were waiting for this your whole career. Your reputation's gone to the dogs. Now, what you gonna do about it?"

"Sorry can I just squeeze past and get my handbag please—"

"You cut their facking hands off."

NULLEST; VOIDEST; DEADEST MEAT

He waits near the front of the nave staring at melting glass, wondering is there still time to piss. Could he stall proceedings he asks the crucifix in his head— there is none in this ruined church, no ceiling, no one truly alive. It stands the wrong way round. He thinks he can hold it in, that he doesn't want to look like he's doing a runner. He looks at his missing feet, the compass legs of old. Mammy is sat at the front all smiles and no pulse. She keeps fiddling with her hat, her face moving in different frames of ageing, mouthing vowels each time he looks. He's nervous, not sure of his own age. Hologram guests sit behind her. Bullies from school, shafted investors, Jeff with the noose still attached, his wife and the girl he picked up once whose legal age he guessed. "Hey mister why are you shaking. You just need to relax," she'd said, hand on his thigh before his panicked pull-over. She's chatting to his dad sitting next to her, dead and bloated still. Billy suddenly remembers the ring, did he buy one, where's it gone, was it a dream? He frisks, heart throbbing.

"It's alright Billy, I've got it," a whisper says behind him. It's one of the Abcat's burned boys he last saw alight, spitting like a Catherine Wheel. "Don't worry, Billy. I know it wasn't your fault. What were we doing there, eh? Us perverts behind the times. We should've known better. We had screens of tanned mise en abymes in our own homes. You did my parents a favour. We should get together and crack one out for old time's sake." The boy grins burned gums framed by slapdash, peeling grafting. "Although you might have to do the honours for me." He reveals the ring, glowing like a new horseshoe in his charred, fingerless hand. The boy looks up. Snow kisses his skinned phantom face.

"What am I doing here," says Billy. "I'm a spare prick at a wedding."

"You can't get cold feet now old chap," says the boy. "Snow Angel's arrived." Lucy, veiled in red, glides down the aisle to strains of Ave Maria. Dead mammy lives inside each vibrato, she shakes and weeps in cold sound. Billy starts to piss slowly, releasing broken glass. Hell lives here.

"Well that was all a bit much," says Lucy later, crossing the threshold.

"I don't think this is the bridal suite," Billy drops her onto the single bed, "but it'll do." He peels the veil from her myxomatosis eyes.

"Help me," says the weeping Madonna, her body hard against the mustard velour headboard. The lone bulb blinks and hides decaying colour. The room stained and dark.

"Wait a second." Billy gets up, shirtless, opens the curtains out onto to a moonlit car-park filled with rusting fridges. "That's better." He stands at the foot of the bed. "I've wanted this forever. The Duchess was just an entrée. Actually, wait Angel, I need to

piss. Sorry, it's my cystitis. I'll be right back, beautiful."
Hairy toes tongue shoes with their backs broken.
There is no light. He waits at the top of the stairs,
guessing their depth and the fall that might gulp
him. Something else is there with him, alive, silent.
A dragging without words in front of him. He stops
breathing and waits. What is the weight there? A
smothering with no edge. He senses meat, sweat,
physical exertion. Slides his hand into his pocket for
the neon lighter. There's no easy way to mime fire.
He must gamble alone here. "Hello?' he offers to
blackness. He waits again, his thumb pronouncing
heat. Count to five. In the dark again, a rumination.
Heavy dragging. A pursed exhale like a complaint
about noise shimmied under a door. Furniture
removal … at this time? He thinks of proud mammy
and his bride and the pain in his bladder. Jesus is
watching, Jesus must blast thunder into any badness
here. One last light.

Bald head beneath, turning fast. "Billy!" He drops the
lighter but all is clear in the dark. His heart bolting—its
breaking in a gone dream. "Let bygones be bygones
pal, I could do with your help." Mad Sinbad, all cue
ball and teeth, match in hand. His slaughter grin
staying put. Don't body buckle wild, not ever or now.
"I'm trying to carry this down the stairs." A black bin
bag, a crumpled bulk at his feet. "Take hold of the
end. Careful you don't trip." Don't disappoint, don't
fall. Lucy will wait. He knows its contents, he knows
too well the horror that sinks to the bottom of canals.

THE WOMEN'S REGRET; THE MEN'S REGRET

"Billy. Are you watching or wot." She'd been the kind of playing child who'd stuff sand in her clunge. A little older, she said her mother danced with the devil then someone's house burned down. She was certain but couldn't settle on the colour of her mother's dress. Or whose house it was. These days it had to be theirs. Mum stayed inside, indifferent to any fire not in her mouth. Flames around her flames. Her ashy ruin a secret club, the password up in the air. Dad was still gone; nowhere.

Billy stared into nothing in front of him. He wore a ratty towel over his shoulders. He thought this was what dance teachers did in films he hadn't seen. Serious Europeans; strict Austrians in black who give heavy-handed lessons about death and piano. Cold soup you don't sip warm. *Gaz-patch-oh. Oh, Lucy. I don't want anything more. No other.* He'd built her a wooden track to skate on. It curled around the cinema, up the aisle and past the bogs. His crotchless angel would take flight in love-struck circles.

Mum was still in bed at this point but helped in her own way. She could manoeuvre her smoking mouthful hands-free now, tonguing what was necessary. Her nimble claws sewed womby drapes to hide the cinema's damp. Lucy came home to a pile of red and sympathy in smoke signals. She sobbed on the bog.

Billy had his heart set on Lipizzan stallions so staked out livestock auctions. The best animals he could afford were clapped out, saggy-backed, sad-eyed glue fodder. He ended up buying a pair of donkeys, two tired sisters with scarred flanks. They wore cracked bridles with bright seaside-themed nameplates. Delighted with his purchase, Billy rushed back to London with them in the back of his transit van, its muffler dragging. Sandy and Shell's sorry hooves smudged yesterday's news on the papered floor. They peered out on the slow lane at lights low in fog. Their ghost faces mooned waving kids and a bemused bride in a wedding cortege, her own face a bad smell in the back of a rented car. There had been a third sister, Star, who hadn't made it to market. She was the smallest of the three with a white forehead flash. Despite her size, she'd bent faithfully under fat kids and trundled furthest across Blackpool sand. She was kindest to the unsure child and stayed still when saddled. But none of this dented her indentured servitude. Like Ted before her, she ended in a leaky stagger in a paddock, a soft puzzled muzzling from her sisters.

INVERTED YEARNING

"Billy these aren't horses. And I'm not the bleedin Virgin Mary."

"Don't talk like that Angel. We need to play to the crowd. They're family friendly. Everyone loves a nativity scene."

What did you expect? Old gummed Billy trying hard to root new teeth. When the gums are gone there's nothing left, never mind what's there. You have to look past that now. Lucy's not standing still, even in sleep. And him—that old fool—well he's never not queuing up with the wolves at wrong doors, waiting for meat confetti. The tiny rotten bits meant for birds. Mum was in on it, aware. She had bitter words to say in smoke letters, winter language on windows. Regret was pruning her like a cold bath. Steve was doing well now; in charge of the lit letters on *Wheel of Fortune*. Mum could smoke of nothing else. *Only the consonants, mind. They won't trust that cunt with the vowels.* He was snapped falling out of one of Mad Sinbad's clubs with a glazed gameshow hostess. A young tottering thing with a velcro mouth. "Bet she loves it up the arse," said mum and a look that said there was nothing more to say. Her speech ceased after that. Her life counted down in final nails—happy times compared to this freshly staked hell. She was done with it. The weight was sharp, digging in everywhere tender. She couldn't stand his success, her own sashaying stink.

Knee deep in wound, the dead rising. The donkeys' exclamation mark ears impaled gestures in wet. The Victorian drains started to bleed a Styxian oxbow of piss and spunk, the cinema's tell-tale heart. Shell and Sandy, installed in strawed toilet cubicles, were now honking sundials yelling bad time, the kind that says this isn't getting any better for a good while yet. "I can't practice with them carrying on like that. It's a farce," said Lucy.

Billy rolled his sleeves and told her to go for long walks. "If I see you cunts back here before dark I'll turn you all into salami."

She led the sisters in circles past the last of Soho's pubs, pawnshops and clip-joints. Market stall holders donated their best apples while walk-up girls chimed from top windows. Worried johns washed their knobs in sinks: "Who's outside? What you laughing at?" Lucy pulled her collar up. What if someone from work saw her? She stood staring outside a dance shop, the donkeys' leads slack in her hands. Young straw-hatted girls giggled past, laden with pink slippers and their mothers' pushy dreams. *That was me once.* Sandy and Shell kept their heads bowed. Rain poured into gaping hours.

Our fields are finished. They've fallen into the sea.

Those useless parts of us, pearled hardness at the back of your mouth and the dormant worm in your gut. They telegram each other, weighing the smoke and the dirt and their revenge in explosion and ache. The truth about you could only be stomached by early man in ae chunks, when there was nothing hard to say, nothing aflame on the tip of the tongue. It got swallowed whole without tearing. Early man was an antebellum sort with a singing sky at the back of his mouth. Don't believe the basic grunts, the hair-pulls, the crude tools, the soft stone sex lozenges they show you. "Oooh they were just like us," you coo in the queue for the next exhibit. It was all song; sonorous circles lifted from birds. There were no cuts, no consonants, no closures. The sounds were the soft underbelly of a mother's tongue. Experience without day or playing dead. Lucy's mother had tried her best to say this, her smoky vowels a reassurance, a hoarseness that comes after reminiscing through the night. They're called late talkers these days, non-thrashers in sentences. Some are just sussing their loss.

Such a beautiful dream at last: Lucy's steadfast contortion lit by blue. Billy sullen with a towel round his neck, fag in mouth, trying to work a camera. "What if the wind changes Billy. Please hurry up." The cinema was clean and stank of stale pine. The donkeys were being looked after by a runaway with bad eyes who dished out dodgy change in amusement arcades. The coins mattered by weight; their faces didn't count.

That's how it is in the dark.

The teen boy—Terry—was too thin and always gripping something as if he might blow away. When it wasn't a donkey lead it was one of Lucy's slips or capes. "I've just sewed a nice new trim on the bottom, hope you don't mind." Any clothing left down for a second, even Billy's towel, was instantly customized with ruche or appliqué. The work was delicate, precise. Within a week, Sandy and Shell had been transformed into piñatas.

The boy helped in other ways. He read Lucy's palm and made her disappear further inside corsets. "I could touch the sides now," he said and they laughed. He showed her his own bound chest and scars. They talked girths and scissors, lengths and legendary buckets. He kept the landlord's visits secret, his faraway gaze ubac. With mum ensconced in smoke, Lucy was in charge of this part of the business—the nuts and bolts and bolted doors. She shooed Billy out of the building and spritzed her room with perfume. She was nervous, pacey, and needed Terry to re-do her shaky hand's work. He combed her hair as they both blew smoke at cracked glass. "My nerves are bad tonight, don't leave me. Pass me the big honkers will you?" Terry pierced the earrings' stalks gently through grouped skin. A little blood mixed with glint. "That's the worst part of the night done with, I promise." Lucy trusted him; he was always right. But to reassure her, he climbed inside the wardrobe with a gripped broom and waited.

THE DANCES WE DID BETWEEN ROCKS AND HARD PLACES

An eyeless spy hides. He's seen the end so rests his head against a dead fox. Old fur warms even ghosts' stubborn skin. He keeps his breath gilled—silent—above uncracked bone. He wonders why he bothers when there's nothing to guess, no outcome unknown.

Sitting on the single bed, Lucy adjusts the gash in her gown. A perfunctory valley, where *hiraeth* imbues her scent and tears. She thinks of dad somewhere in the fields, off the map, shapeless. *Dad sounds like god. Dog. Backwards. Shapeless daddy. All-seeing.* It's up to her to bring him home, to make mum flameproof. She wants fame. Clear-eyed rabbits. Fast feet on a drunk orbit. "Come in," she says, unconvinced.

Sinbad dips under the doorframe, hands rubbing his bouldered sides. "I'm not disturbing am I."

"Course not," says Lucy. She decides half an hour. If she spaces out her words can she pad it out to primped nothing? Cheap meat pumped with water. *Yes. Half an hour is that.* But the clingy wrapping must be unsheathed first. "You can sit on the bed if you like." She pats blankets, her first wind-up gesture. Will she vomit or just feel like it. Sinbad ignores her. He picks up glass ornaments then places them elsewhere, anti-clockwise. He acts new to touch—

wary. Lucy sees a trail of slime and wonders if love can ever evolve from languidness. He pauses at a crystal horse. "My dad got me that." *Wrong answer.* She loosens her silk belt.

"How is the old man," Sinbad says. Bobbing glance. Nowhere is taking too long. Nowhere is a fat stubborn thing.

"Away. Dowsing."

"So it's still just you and your mum then." He sits next to Lucy on the bed, still holding the ornament.

She unties the belt, the soft valley opens. *It's spring.* Sneaking puffiness nudges Terry's new trims. "I know we're behind but it's hard," she says. "We've got big plans. We'll always have the brand. We just need time. We just need time. Mum's been talking about a commemorative zoetrope—"

"Take it off." The gown falls. Sinbad fingers the animal's inflections. Her hands console each other, naked; flood-lit. Both waiting in a deli counter queue, strangers with close numbers. Fat font barking under fluorescent light. He likes his meat with a face. "Why don't you like me," he asks. Terry in hiding tongues the fox's snout. He sees its last stand and the hounds and gaze and grudge that stain the field.

"I think you're a lovely man, Sinbad. Really lovely." Her blood twitches, flooding faster. She smells sweat. *Cunts must try hard to come; Terry knows all aches.* He bets on her dugs, either chapel hat pegs or splayed roses. He's never wrong about anatomy.

"Not like that though," Sinbad says, his fingers now on the ears, tweaking.

"We're still getting to know each other," says Lucy.

His hard hands now on legs. "Is it cos of my head. It's sweaty isn't it? You think I look old."

She counts three Mississippis and pictures the journey of sedimentary rock into safe tepidness and unending sea with no memory. She decides to risk it, to toe muddy waters. Her hand now on his cheek, firm, unsympathetic. His eyes still shut. He grabs and slow burns her wrist. "Lie back."

I've seen your sort milling about; cannibals pacing in the wings while us parasites take soft turns to keep our bellies in the warmth.

Sinbad holds the figurine firm and blinks too much, quick shutter releases past seeing. Lucy lies stunned, legs open for business. The animal slips over her skin, four tiny hooves cold kisses. Up downy arms and the longer hairs common on the backs of girls' thighs. She stares, lips letting out wider breaths, behind them nothing, no gut there. Hooves on chipped nails she hides in winter. Ropey veins a busy sun knows and sees through. She can't see if the horse has eyes. *What does Terry really see with that thick grin of his. Some kind of kink in soft focus. Dave's prime cut away from the picture. That's where life is.* Sinbad's mouth stays shut, his trajectory steady. The horse wanders over scars and pocks, dips in her belly. She laughs; it stops. Sinbad fumbles with one hand still on glass. *She saw him coming.* Spindly counts budge nothing of bulk and do not make the unmade bed. Lucy's at a loss, feeling smaller. He rams it home hard. The figurine's head woodpecking. An animal mouth protesting at its consonant future. She sounds like her mum, always nagging something nearing vague. All daughters become their mothers. Those were never odds.

•

"Dad?"

"No echo."

"Did he say that?"

"There was never a grudge."

"Here?"

"Not here. Between other regions."

"But where?"

"After wet."

"Ice?"

"Don't try to see it moving."

•

I knew my number—its strains and curves. It was stuck on my front and back and held everything up. I was scared if it fell off they'd have to mop me up. The glittered fringe strands my mum rose early to divide. She pulled hard on my skewed plait and my smile slid. We did our best but accepted it. In the final touches I looked at the pale brush of fur on her lip. Was she a secret yeti at night, changing back in time for breakfast? The morning was charged with possibility. When she combed to the sky I stood tip-

*toed in light. I forgave her everything. I did not need
to remember my lines; I had them tattooed on my
pink bits. Dad drove off early with an evil exhaust, 'I
wish my wife was this dirty,' fingered in the windows'
dust. That's what it's like down there when you get
old, after all the young cobwebs have grown.*

Hi Lucy,

Can we have a chat in private? Does 2pm this
afternoon work for you?

Regards,
Rivis

Dave, is it ok if we don't go to the pub for
lunch later? Rivis wants to speak to me in
private at 2!! Don't know what it could be
about :s Cheers, L

No worries. What did he say?

Just could we have a chat in private. I'm worried—

Don't be, its probly just about moving u onto
a later shift or something. He wanted a private
chat with me about my earring … I told him to
bugger off and stop disrespecting my culture.

Why didn't he say anything in the email though?

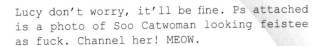

Lucy don't worry, it'll be fine. Ps attached
is a photo of Soo Catwoman looking feistee
as fuck. Channel her! MEOW.

Dave xx

My sweat leaked through small gasped whorls in my
skin. I pretended to hear Dave's anecdote about the
time he leaned in to kiss Soo Catwoman at a gig but
was stopped by a glass bottle smashing his head,
his bloody tears sprouting joy. It was the most erotic
moment of his life, he said. Nothing had touched it
since.

I yanked my earphones out and stood up, heavier
at my desk. I hurried to the bog. Chose the furthest
one from the door, next to a woman eating crisps
and arguing with her boyfriend on the phone. I felt
invisible compared to her gratuitous multi-tasking. I
unfolded a small triangle of card carefully, undressing
its secret white navel. It was less conspicuous than
a baggie, more ritualistic. I paused. Sadness and
insistence duelled then joined glad sides. Two cold
slugs went up my nose all business no kissing I could
not deny any of it. *Oh god. Oh fuuuuuuuck.*

I sat down, squeezing my hands between knees that
were surely losing their bones, and the bones their
conviction. "I think I'd be ok," I reckoned. "I'd make
something out of being jelly." My thoughts were
tender clippings talking over each other, ecstatic
forgettings travelling hard through my inside's
ravages. The burn merely confirmed everything was

ok; I'd found myself here, alive, listening to a woman eating crisps and breaking up with her boyfriend on the bog. New revving entrenched in me, a catapult taut in my breast. I flushed the toilet then heated my unwashed hands in a hot blast.

Rivis took his time smudging the door shut against new carpet. He was doughy; a heavy wheezer. My knuckles frisked my nostrils. "Horrible day out there isn't it," he said, not looking at me. Rain on his skin. Sweat? He was the type to move in a congealed force-field, bleeding beige on unlucky neighbours on buses.

I would prop my sad weight against all of this. I coughed a dead "yeah".

Rivis cleared his own throat. "Right Lucy, I'm not gonna beat around the bush. This is to do with your monthly performance. You've fallen way behind the rest of the team ..."

I couldn't hear him. He was a vanitas sweating talk at me, a reminder of what my dad would never be. The rabbits were the same. However sore their brooding, I'd never find their corpses or the desperately clinging. I'd never trip over stiff fur no matter how far I ran. And I'd never cry over dad. I was proud of the rabbits' form of exposure, their glassy self-respect. There'd be no wounded wailing in the night. Their exit was neat; egoless. Their bodies buried in deserts, the hurt quickly effaced. *That's how it's done.* Me and mum would cope just fine. I could be anyone in the dark, any age. I'd collapse into dense clots, refusing food and sky. Draw dad's shadow on my bedroom wall and spend my nights recreating his voice and that'd be enough. That's all people were anyway—bones picked from dictionaries. I dwelled on this as Rivis displayed graphs with red lines belly-flopping fast. I wanted to punch through rooms I suspected but could not see. I'd keep my arm straight and smash through walls and urinals and out onto the street. I maintained my nodding as I framed him thrown off his swivel chair, his belly breaking Taiko waves. "I'll definitely make it up next month," I lied, my pulse at hard speed. My teeth and thighs clenched. There was now another face in the room between us. It was still Rivis but younger, gauzey, the redness drained. His cheeks were an astronaut's first time in space, all slo-mo serenity.

"You've been late five times this month Lucy. Every time I look over you're yawning or chatting to Dave."

"I'm really sorry. It won't happen again," I said, unsure which word to stress. Maybe I was giving him the eye without knowing. Maybe I was naked, frigging myself and confessing to an unsolved murder. I couldn't be sure of anything in this room. I repeated bland words and between sameness it snagged. I'd seen that face before, up close. An opiated floating above me. I felt horror and liquid. Was the new tang blood, a leaky ceiling, his sweat? Had I bit my lip off? Was it dripping down my chin as Rivis politely busied himself with pointing at my productivity freefall? I skimmed the table for red dew. Had I seen him at the cinema, or were my nerves and the lines—both his and the ones exploding in my bloodstream—scrambling, mouthing promises to each other i couldn't hear or keep? I made no sudden movements; my nods were slow anchors videotaped backwards. Dad would be so disappointed. Everything below my neck felt like a balloon with no knot. I was scared I'd dart into corners and stick against the walls' fresh paint. There'd be no punch lines in the wreckage; no recovery position I could cold-call. Maybe it was a test before a softer reality ... maybe Rivis had wired the room up to sense the truth about me ... maybe every surface was polygraphic. I prised my fingers from the table into my dumb wet lap. "Lucy. Lucy, are you ok?" My grin rinsed the last of my sweat.

•

Loss gave us our first voice, a diffused place, formless like bat formation. On closer inspection they were heavier bodies, their spans wider. They could've been albatrosses but never got close. They circled for years until sublated, picking us off like meteors with heavy grudges. Thirst did the rest. We couldn't tell what kind of luck it was—had the dinosaurs gone through this, our grandmothers before us? There was no parole. We moved in a slow phalanx, our frowns carved. Our passion was violent but strained, heavy-lidded. We were sad totems, sinking into the dirt we'd boldly claimed as our own. Our young set off for towns and cities, for houses with windows. They forgot the words we taught them. We knew the mild climate would not last. We did not know where we'd be buried; our consonants carried further cold snaps that pushed us on. They were finer, gristled. Dry animal sounds, the blockage of breath with the negative at work. We submitted to its henpecking. We were sure there were pyramids we could live in where the sky met the sea. This wasn't the salt talking; we'd seen them in waiting room magazines. We stammered in the cold for our dead and our daughters who would not return, insulted by their dowries, what they must have meant to us. Our voices both carried the pulseless and pitted us against them. They were all we had left in the wind. We needed fresh water. We were dragging ships across dry land. We walked so we'd gain distance and not die with the dead.

•

"You need to put a hot flannel on it and go see a doctor."

"It's fine Angel, really."

"Billy, it's infected. You can't walk around with a gammy thigh."

"It's nothing, just an ingrown hair. We don't have time for this." Our wounded king pulled his trousers up. The flooding had cleared in the cinema, but opening night was closing in and none of his grand plans had been realized. Lucy kept changing her routine, adding curlicues, terser circles. "Angel, all you have to do is show your snatch. I don't know why you're getting so worked up about it," Billy said after another failed Salchow, another messy loop. He stubbed out his cigarette and limped to the back room. She couldn't win. Every extra run-through meant another late start at work, more time for mum to self-immolate, more chance of a run-in with Mad Sinbad and a glass animal. But if the routine was perfect—and a choreographer happened to be in the audience—it could be the start of dizzy stardom, the West End, roses in her dressing room from anonymous admirers. She had it all mapped out. Terry would take charge of the house affairs, the furnishings, her stock market investments. Dad would pop round for tea in the Orangery, the afternoon sun dappling their laughter and antique doilies. Dave would be cajoled from clumsy butlering into a sit down and a cup of tea to reminiscence about the ruins they'd climbed over. The past would become dead language.

The dismal sound of now soon cut through the dream. Mum could not be left to burn the street down. Under a late shroud Lucy parked a wheelbarrow outside the house then snuck upstairs. Even in sleep mum still chugged away, an industrial piston in electrical time, dead-set on progress regardless of where it might lead.

Across slow dawn Lucy wheeled the little sparrow through the city. They skipped the backstreets for the smooth tarmac of empty dual carriageways and elegant city planning. Their journey to the cinema was tracked by a bored nightshift CCTV operator on an industrial estate. The man—a creased sort on a swivel chair—kept himself awake with supermarket-brand energy drinks and a blinking MILF chat window on his phone. He imagined the MILF was also a lonely shift worker, marooned in an economic backwater or stale bedroom with the curtains drawn til afternoon. At his sleepiest, he'd wonder if they stopped pretending to be *oldslag69* and *yunghungstud* ... could there be some kind of shared revelation that'd change their lives for the better? Maybe they'd meet and say the things they were never able to say to anyone real in their lives. It was sad warmth for him, like spooning with a stranger before a walk of shame home.

Lucy and mum pit-stopped at petrol stations for cigarettes, the lop-sided barrow pulling in behind lorries with exotic number plates. It was the only thing to keep mum from howling—the promise of a cigarette bath to buffer her bones against the cold.

"What's she doing back here," said Billy, staring at Lucy bathing her mother in ashy water.

"We're looking after her," said Lucy. "She's as much a part of this business as me."

"Well get Terry to take care of her. You've got to nail that Lady Godiva entrance."

Terry made the little sparrow a fireproof smoking jacket with glow in the dark trims and elbow patches. She was put with the donkeys, her fag bouquet dressing the floor in sparks that their hooves stamped out like angry castanets.

Billy decided that if Lucy's mother was not to be moved, she had better start earning her keep. He was twitchy about having her around after the Abcat horror—the smell of burns that always woke him from his worst dreams. She was too frail and dried up for the stage; too mute to be a hostess. Eventually her usefulness became clear to him. With no money from the bank manager and the little of his own gyzymed on Lucy's skates and costumes, there was none to be had for staging, props or special effects. Now they had a smoke machine, pumping her wares at full pelt from the wings. Terry kept the bouquet in full bloom with imitation fags bartered from corner shop counters. She seemed to pump faster during Lucy's practices, her plumes reaching higher on fat swells of maternal pride.

•

We were way out, miles off the map. Our men buried in deserts behind us. Put yourself in our shoes, that tread no humus, just dead-ends that force us to traipse backwards through blank prairies, ceaseless famines past all guessed horizons. We can't tell when night ends, if it does.

Our mother tongue was beautiful. We held onto that. The strokes looked like courting dancers or elegant hands discussing weather. Stray hairs swiped from lovers' faces. Our mothers taught us to write in secret for keeps, embroidered in cloth and painted on paper fans in days when we had lipstick, or enough to eat. The code was not for fathers, sons, nor husbands. It was not their talk—that was boxy and bold. We stayed upstairs and did our chores: sewing, spinning, laughing til we burnt their dinners and disguised it with greens. Neighbour girls learnt together, pinching each other when grandmother's back turned. We guessed our wedding nights and giggled. We prayed to wake with teeth, to bite it off, to eat our way out of there. It was sometimes sung, the sorrow of our lot, our aches, our snipes at neighbours. We spelt third day missives, given to our daughters on their happiest days, our saddest til now. Our daughters forced to leave their childhood homes, the safest upstairs space. We knew the emperor had made the wrong rules.

Sometimes we think we must be dead; it'd make the walk so much easier. At least they can no longer call us feudal spies with our mysterious swipes. We think perhaps there is no water, there never was. Maybe we're walking in circles. Now we write our grief on bones and tortoise shells. It won't be buried with us. One day you'll find it on a beach with the bottoms of your trousers rolled, your pastiness squinting at a hard sun. Maybe we're just echoes mixed with sand. Beside a well, one does not thirst. Beside a sister, one does not despair.

•

FLYER WITH PICTURE OF LUCY BENDING OVER WEARING SILVER ROLLERSKATES. THEY APPEAR TO BE SHOOTING LAZERS. SHE IS ALL TEETH, LONG GLUED-ON HAIR ORIGINATING FROM VIRGINS IN RUSSIAN VILLAGES WHO BAWLED ON THEIR 16TH BIRTHDAYS. THEY DID NOT EAT CAKE. SHE IS WEARING KNICKERS. MORE TANNED THAN IN THE FLESH, AND UNVEINED. THE TEXT WAS WRITTEN BY BILLY IN HIS ARM CHAIR, THE SUM OF £9.47 AND €0.01 DOWN ITS SIDES. HE WAS EATING HIS DINNER AT THE TIME, WATCHING A TV PROGRAMME ABOUT THE AMAZING FEATS OF DISABLED DOGS IN WHEELCHAIRS. HE LAUGHED THEN STOPPED LAUGHING, THEN DECIDED IF ANYONE

COULD LAUGH IT WAS HIM WITH ALL THE LUCK HE'D HAD. HE ATE ONE PIECE OF BURNT TOAST WITH CHEESE ON IT, THE OTHER HONEY. WASHED BOTH DOWN WITH TEA. THE MILK HAD SCUM ON THE TOP BUT SMELT OK SO WAS CHANCED. HE THEN BUTTONED HIS SHIRT COLLAR AND SAT STRAIGHT AND GOT DOWN TO BUSINESS, HIS BETTING SHOP BIRO WRITING THE FOLLOWING:

★

FUN FOR ALL THE FAMILY

THE DISCERNING GENTLEMAN'S CHOICE

BRING YOUR HOTEL KEY FOR FREE ENTRY

SKATING

HAS NEVER BEEN THIS SEXY

BEAT WEST END TICKET PRICES

SEE SEXED UP VERSIONS OF MUSICAL HITS

GLAMAROUS FREE SHOE SHINE SERVICE

STUNTS YOU WOULDN'T BELIEVE

PETTING ZOO   MULTIPLE FIRE EXITS

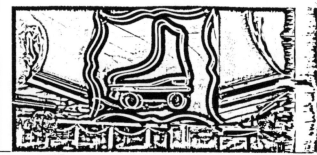

"Mate. I can't print that, sorry." A ponytailed man. Late twenties. Leaning on counter. Psychedelic cannabis-leaf screensaver on phone next to him.

"What do you mean you can't print it?"

"We don't print that sort of thing here." Nails scratching goatee. *Cht-cht-cht.* Looks drawn on but trimmed daily.

"It says you do flyers in the windows. Professional shiny ones."

"Yeah, yeah we do." Half-arsed hand gesture. It's not mid-week yet. Not yet midday.

Billy scrapes lip's dead skin. Nervous tic well grooved. "Well what's wrong with this then." Young man sniffs. Nose rub improv. "Is it spelt wrong? I can change any mistakes."

Both sides wait. The phone rings. Tinny hip-hop hit. *Pointless.* "Sorry," the younger man says. Retreats to the back room.

Billy inspects his work. Holds it close to his face. *Something he missed?* "Yes mate I'm hiding in plain sight alright. Jeeeeesus. I'm so stoned I can't feel my eyes." Billy waits. Looks at posters for dance events. Charity galas. STRICTLY NO PARKING signs. "Yeah we had a table and everything. Grey Goose, champagne, the lot. Won't be eating for a month now haha." Billy examines the letter sizes, wondering if the shop does the Snellen charts in hospitals, is it a lucrative business, does it move with the times. "Bro she was so far in my face I could smell the sea. The owner even sat with us cos of how much we were spending. Really nice guy. Was well gangster, the old skool kind. Said if I did some flyers for him he'd get us in for free." Billy gulps and calls out. "Can you hurry up please I'm in a rush."

Young man all elbows. "Sorry mate but we won't print that."

Billy flustered, counting the letters, peeling tiles, posters, focusing on his anxious tricks. "Is it the formatting? I can get rid of the lazers if that'd help; they're just there to create a feeling of space and timelessness."

Chin stroke opposite. Jaw adjusting for terms and conditions. "Sorry, but we don't print strip club flyers, tart cards, any derogatory stuff. Company policy." Phone swipe. Two new messages. Uppercase letters. Exclamation like a terrible accident.

"Excuse me, I think you've got the wrong idea." *He can't see the shakes he can't see the shakes he can't see the shakes*. Flyer back on counter. "This has nothing to do with a strip club. It's an artistic night-life establishment showcasing the best in musical dance and exotica." *What does exotica even mean you eejit*. Focus now on subduing redness. *Picture icebergs. Kate Winslet's nips in the Titanic. Bollocks*.

"It's not The Nut Cracker mate, is it?" More rueful goatee stroking.

"I ... I ... you clearly don't understand. You don't understand art. You don't understand fuck all." *Oh Jesus he can see everything.* Floundering Billy sees the disabled dogs in their chariots, a canned laugh track peppering their falls into flowerbeds. *Amazing feats? Were they fuck.*

"Mate"—all I'm-doing-you-a-favour hands—"this is amateur hour anyway. Look at this shit! You're wasting your time."

Blood and water boil at the same temperature then boil over, be sure of that boyo. Billy's finger so close now it nears the longer hairs unseen in the morning's nausea. "Ah so you're an expert are you. Well what do you know about the Mapes eh. What do you know about the one-foot double Salchow. What about the cunting Lutz eh. Or maybe you're an expert on the Mohawk."

"Sorry bruv you've lost me." "See! Fuck all!" Billy in full shake now.

"I think you should try somewhere else."

"Keep making your silly signs for the blind!" No one's listening! *Uarrrrrrrrrrrrrrrgh. Sense man for bleeding sake make some sense for once.* Tipped into fugue, lighter in hand, peeling a "Bob and Sue's 50th anniversary party! (parking at rear)" poster from the counter. He lights a corner. "See! You're nothing! You know nothing!" Bloody lips from too hard a scrape. He runs out of the shop with the poster in his hand, Bob and Sue going up in smoke.

MATCHSTICKS AND THE SIZE OF THE DECEASED'S EYES

"He thinks he's Nijinksy."

"Nah, he's Dianna Ross."

"All fur coat no knickers."

"They say the new George Balanchine."

"A soft-figured creature."

"A shameless shirt-lifter."

The men took turn to pot balls and sip light ale in squeaky leather. Graham was among them, leaning across for the longest shots, *scusing me* to women squeezing past on their way to the toilets. They'd grown up together. They'd picked on the same supply teachers and unzipped their virginities with the same girls behind unlit working men's clubs. They were thorough but never chatterboxy. They did not grass.

Lager was used to help vertebrae loosen over green baize, to spill tension from their day's tedium. It was sunk in eager silence. Sometimes they talked about their children; whether university or learning a trade was better. Jokes did not require impressive punchlines; it was all in the telling til it was *time gentlemen please*. Billy had grown up on the same street but they always considered him an outsider, useful only for making up football team numbers or testing the depth and toxicity of local swamps. He didn't have the right trainers, English parents or pubes until too late on. When their rounds of Knock Knock Ginger escalated into minor breaking and entering, Billy would be the first pushed through small gaps, hedgerows or into dead-end paths trimmed with shadows and barks. His dragging leg always got him caught, tangled in wire or thin air. This never amounted to more than a telling off from his mum or bed without dinner. That was until the funeral buffet incident.

•

Mr Gibbons lived opposite Billy's shabby terrace in a wattle and daub cottage. He was an elderly, well-ironed sort, always smartly turned out and with a spare kind word. His cottage had won various awards for its authentic thatch roof and sensitive upkeep. It even appeared on the front of a home magazine, which Gibbons neatly cut out and sellotaped to his front door, next to Yorkshire Terrier and Neighbourhood Watch stickers. He was a proud gardener and beekeeper, while his wife led the recorder class at the local primary school. They had once run the UK's Elvis Presley fan club before burning everything King-related and making a hard turn to religion.

When a blunt death notice for Mrs Gibbons appeared in the local paper, the boys decided she was actually still alive. Her husband had beaten her to near-death with her own recorder, and was keeping her in a coma in one of the cottage's upstairs rooms. The old man was an evil genius who—with the help of his bees—was turning his innocent missus into a royal jelly more powerful than rocket fuel and crude oil combined. The jelly would be sold and consumed at church fêtes across the country, creating an army of human-bee hybrid drones, intent on destroying civilization and turning Buckingham Palace into a headquarter hive. Mr Gibbons would survey the scene from its highest balcony while caressing his villain beard. The peaceful passing from the paper was a cover-up that only the boys could see through.

It was a convenient narrative that carried the boys' sci-fi TV world into the sighing cul-de-sacs outside. It brightened damp, mildew days of long division and waiting for tired mums to return from their cleaning jobs, bleach wafting upstairs to their stickered rooms. Billy was not convinced. His mum had always spoke highly of Mr Gibbons, especially after he gave the family some honey one miserable Christmas. And when Billy wet himself during a recorder rendition of *Lord of the Dance* and had to wear lost property girls' shorts for the rest of the day, it was Mrs Gibbons who drove him home to avoid a walk of shame.

They had detective work to do. Graham decided that the sham funeral would provide the best cover for break-in and discovery of Mrs Gibbon's jellified body. They wouldn't need to be shy about it; after all they'd soon be heroes for mankind and the public good. They wrote down the number of the local newspaper, and while waiting to cross the road, delegated the best quotes. Billy was told he was the strong, silent type.

Graham was in charge of the hammer. He took a dentist's tap to the terriers frosted faces. "Smash em in Gray," instructed the seeping ringleader nicknamed Suvius. The dogs' bowed skulls gave in quick. Inside, the boys' steps took on socked softness. They'd wiped their feet and wore gloves. No one was in but they kept their bodies careful. "You'll need this if you see any bees," said a freckled sort, unzipping a hold-all rammed with cans of fly killer. "Wow, Mrs Gibbons was really fit when she was young." Her framed health in albumen overalls oversaw the congealing scene. The boys dithered at the bottom of the stairs in a sniping whirlpool that would inevitably spit Billy out first.

Upstairs, Suvius kicked open the first door they came to, its slam followed by a karate stance ricocheting down to lukewarm Billy. The crochet-quilted bed was neat and empty. "Where is she then?" said Graham. Their fevered fingers lifted and peeled back surfaces. "Look out for any sticky stuff; she might have been melted down into wax." Worn out his 'n' hers wardrobes vomited moths; cotton flutterings hell-bent on heaven. The freckled lad fumbled fast for cans. "There could be bees in there too!" Empty pill bottles on a bedside table, Mrs Gibbon's swallows counted down. "That's just for show," said Suvius. "She was never ill. Look for the recorder—it'll be bent and have blood on it. And whatever you do don't play it—that'll bring the bees out." On the windowsill sat a family of hand-stitched golliwoggs. The Gibbons never had kids.

Downstairs the boys slumped in straight-back chairs. "This is well boring," said Billy. "Where's the bees?" They spotted the buffet behind them, a large spread with two kinds of mash potato—plain and chived—glooped high. Suvius knew how to win them back. "She's in the food, lads. The royal jelly's in the buffet." He reached for a porcelain dancer and dunked her in deep trifle, a sickly gashing trial just for show. The smaller boys' gasps somersaulted into airy laughs. Braced-smirks masked vigilance, their wait for inevitable violence. Graham, vying for promotion, grabbed egg salad and grinned. "Go on Gray, let's smash it up!"

Mr Gibbons had prepared the buffet himself, partly to save money—most of the couple's savings had gone towards Mrs Gibbons' end-of-life care—and because homegrown vegetables and honey from a garden nurtured by his wife were central to her remembrance and celebration. He wanted to forget the vivid motorways that crawled under her skin. He couldn't see the boys elbow deep in cake, flicking soup at Jesus above the mantelpiece, spraying flabby swastikas on windows. All bee talk had curdled into raging mouthfuls; the sound of a mauling at a garden party, a dog refusing to let go of broken skin. These were boys who often went hungry, waiting for their mums from evening cleaning and conveyor-belting for limp slabs of cold death in scant sauce.

When they heard the key in the door, they scrambled into the kitchen and through the window. Billy was left to pull himself up into the sink, a stringy mess hanging from his mouth. He could hear cooing from the lounge—that serious adult tone reserved for desperate talk or the hushed health of relatives back in Ireland. He agonized his own scatting prayer to god and Jesus and all those lads to help him just this once, he wouldn't tell, he'd start telling the truth in confession and not the storylines in car chase TV.

It was Mr Gibbons who walked into the kitchen first, his face a collapsed house. Billy's mother was not far behind. Hers was worse. Billy was lifted out of the sink stinking and bawling and carried out onto the street, his mum threatening to pull his shorts down and smack him in front of the whole village.

Mr Gibbons was seen little after what happened. He stayed demolished, stroke-like. Occasionally he'd collect his pension in the post office, his stink clearing any queue. Some villagers said he had a skin complaint; that light and soap made it worse. Like Elvis before him, handsome Jesus was thrown out, left waiting by the side of the road. The cottage became a mossy, cracked affair; the garden forgotten. The hive's dying was drawn out. The queenless colony collapsed under a gatecrashed party of feasting wax moths chewing through weakened combs.

•

A red room—furred, a cocky sort—gagged; a devil— of sorts; the scene—exitless; windows—missing; you're a showbiz type are ya, I was in showbiz, must show you my scrapbook sometime; the dog sniffing circles, the matted Maltese; fack he's got a chicken bone, he'll choke on that; a card trick smile; no sun down here; Steve tied up; no heliotropism, it's for your own safety; I've met all the greats; cold sea sweats on Steve's skin; relax mate, I'm just playing with ya; dead satellite; the shakes' shakes; in Japan they're into this rope stuff as a kink; you wouldn't believe the Japanese; the cruelty and precision; you have to admire it; it's for your own safety; can't have trouble upstairs; people just want a good time; you thought you woz a big man; throwing glass into drinks; I've seen you on the telly; champers for the table; taking an age to spell a simple word; never anything important to say; the rope's not too tight is it; it's never about people's lives; some daft phrase; glib abyssing; spilling out my club; the dog nosing a dark corner; getting the girls too drunk; you're a slippery type; a greasy climber; I changed time pal; I've been in the army; I know discipline; crawled naked over glass; see that scar on my chin I sewed it up myself; I was an untrained surgeon; couldn't even sew a button; it's called Darwinism; the weak stay still and get eaten; it's life or death pal so you better keep twitching; that's why the insects have done so well for themselves; champion twitchers; not about punches and bombast lad; I bit hard to get blood on my teeth; came out the womb with my dukes up; saved me over my mother; nah I wasn't on duty; it was an obstacle course, got caught on a wire fence; the future carves itself into flesh; before you know it you're watching Wheel of Fortune in a nappy; why do they need so many legs eh; the future's based on insects isn't it; all cold metal and remote action; calm drones; are the ropes too tight, are you alright mate; still breathing; no fun if you choke; I want us both to enjoy ourselves; I've stared down death; sent it packing boyo; you word smiths; you piss artists; you've never been a contender; you got lucky with the letters; who'd you knob eh; who'd you grease up against; take the gag out I can't hear ya; who's that; sorry mate let me; let's play a game; oi wake up sunshine; choose a category; a category you facking spanner like on Wheel of Fortune; alright I'll choose one; how about phrase; just pick a letter and I'll write it and show you what comes up; you taking the piss; how many phrases have Z in; I'm a fair man now play properly; you're not the big man down here; right, give me a proper letter; no there's no A try again; E that's a good one but only one; no two actually; oi stop looking at the dog and concentrate; I no Is; this is a bit like hangman int it; you know the last man they hanged turns out he did do it; DNA that was; come on another one; S yes sir; four of them; R yes one them; you enjoying it; I am; cheap entertainment compared to upstairs eh; you wouldn't believe the mark-ups; it's all watered down of course; T yes you can have one of them too; and a U; D that's right; one letter left Steve don't let me down; oi I told you stop looking at the dog; no one looks at the dog; he's the guvnor; the matted emperor; the real boss; I ain't no mug when it comes to man but with him I'm a lamb; a pushover; posh treats and diamond collar the lot; but I'm the only one who bites round here; come on Steve show me what you got; what's the phrase; it's a common phrase; you know what the consonant is; that's your speciality; look at me when I'm talking to you; what's the answer then Steve; say it; you in a mood with me now or something; you're in a sulk; still think you're above this now do ya; you only switch it on for the cameras and the dolly birds upstairs; this is where it counts mate; this ain't no picnic; no kumbayas in my club; no deathbed afternoon telly; I'm not paid to wipe your arse; this is bigger than cash prizes; spit it out man; what's the phrase when it's at home; repeat after me; something U S T; D; E; S; S; E; R; T; S; aw you're not playing anymore; stop sulking Steve; I'm not asking a lot; do you make that noise in front of the dolly birds; come on finish the game; come on say it; come on say it; come on say it; black Nosferatu rising up on red wall; temple vein fissure; musth bull revelling; patience in lividness; furred sound's frothy mouthing; can you draw a spleen or pin a donkey's; the urge is here; meteors of man rain straight on pleight; torque by hip; Hindu god arms' sleighting; a crater born; blood spume; a kind of birth; Sinbad doesn't forget; Sinbad remembers his birth; the sprayed Maltese laps its balls.

•

Billy dwelled on latrinalia while adding his own to the scarred door, hoping the difficult movement would soon be gone. With a chewed pen he started scratching in upper case. "Please god let me win this time," he wrote with a coiled full-stop his knuckles white til its dwindled end. Opening night was tonight and he hadn't slept. Coffee avalanched through him with visions of fire and Lucy tripping headfirst into empty seats. He repeated positive affirmations while wiping til sore.

Lucy had been retching for three days. Sometimes she matched mum's chugging rhythms but mostly she trailed off into solitary cadence, a blousy free jazz gagging nerves and toil. "Don't even think about doing that on stage," said Billy. She'd not seen him so agitated. Some of the foreign students who'd been brought in for the chorus line quit due to his incessant chides about their flabby labia. Terry's trims were no longer good enough; the donkeys weren't fit for salami. The cinema was veering into a dour miasma.

"Billy you need to calm down," said Terry. "Go for a walk—clear your head. Come back an hour before show-time."

Billy smoked and walked and thought on the family business. He scraped his knuckles on every surface in reach. What would happen to him and all his disasters that kept their pulses, mouthing *feed me* at inappropriate times? He was too tired for this. Youth had never happened in him, he was sure of that. He didn't know where he was going but presumed he'd never stop jinking, dodgem-like, taking hard hits. When he found himself at the river he was relieved. Nothing had ever come to fruition. Blood was pouring a liquid smile. It would do.

Mammy used to say she'd throw herself in the river if anything happened to the children, but that she could only be happy in the furthest foreign land, away from them all. Billy would lie awake, memorizing the ceiling, wondering what she meant and if he'd always ruin things for her. No one had taught him how to sleep—that you didn't just lie there crying for the pain your mammy said you caused. It was fatigue that mangled his leg he reckoned, his body buckling in darkness when it should have been turning toward the sun heaving itself through curtains.

He held onto the cold rail. *I won't go back.* What's left after water burns? And why couldn't he remember whether those plummeting astronauts ever survived? Could anyone survive the flaming chaos of re-entry and eat a sober breakfast? He'd never managed it. What did widowhood look like from up there? No one remembered his first word or the time he was born. Not even mammy in her drunken and most loving moments. Maybe only Laika howled the truth in the silent heat, the world a thrown ball in a mean game.

As he remembered his own burns and shivers after the Abcat gutting, he spotted a white mass in water. He rubbed his eyes red as it got close. It was a dog— but not Laika. A fighting kind, afloat. Its rippling muscles against the colour of money, a bloating green with who knows what disease, what remnants of a good time. How long had it been there, bleak slate and big gash, a downcast leaning against stark odds sunning themselves? Its hairless arse arched up toward indifference and passing traffic. Was the water cold, was it the shock that killed? Had he let her down at the end? The last phone call and goodbye. What was there left to say? With fire you fear the wrong thing.

Back at the cinema Lucy and Terry were putting final touches to moves and trims. A handful of stringy teen runaways had stayed, track-marked and immune to Billy's fat catcalls. They had nowhere else to go. They kept their backs tight to walls, their smiles vapid. They drew on cartoon Cleopatra eyes, violent smears for lips, the wrong thing said all over their gaunt faces. They made Sphinx cardboard headdresses for Sandy and Shell. Mum was painted gold and blue and put in a corner. Billy—defeated—sighed at the last minute Egyptian theme. *They could at least have done the fucking Celts.*

With a dirty towel around his neck, he ushered the cast into a circle.

•

We dreamt of cobalt, rills, glaucous, but never azure, goading azure—it reminded us always of hereness, the lack of water, the ongoing search for something shifting. The sky doesn't end where the sea does, it just pecks at it sometimes, a soft nuzzle that doesn't carry the care you thought. If we could leave our bodies down we would. Clichés and gravity keep us above soil, above the dirt that clings to our nails. We would like to tongue our shadows' holes, to hide there, or any place that would let us in and die in the dark, oneness with no body, hating this bleak kind of ecstasy that spills over. Fly away Peter, fly away Paul, leave the years to softly pass our girly bodies. The walls shout back heat at the filthy sun. The regret we daren't name in the cooling down after. Against a soft crescent, we console ourselves that in this dry place our blood runs faster than any water. If we could find our husbands' graves in the flatlands we would lift our skirts above them. Serried anguish; the skin cells and potsherd we scattered. The vidette—somewhere—presumed dead, scare-crowed. Horizontal hold; vertical hold.

THE PAIN WAS EVER NEW UNDER POURING VATS OF SKY (burn unit)

Amber-veined Lucy waits neither hot nor cold no climate adjusting her plans for flowers and waiting chauffer tapping piano on steering wheel set aside the Orangery with daddy now her deadest dream descending slowly pacing herself in back room a kohled runaway in black shroud mans the front door change in tin it all adds up in desperate times coppers prised from sticky floors by teen making fresh start her regional accent and agony flensed with black tar and the big city Billy has draped the place with what the sparrow deftly made a pink demolishing of place covering dark lisps the doors open for the first time in months bouncers down alley raising their eyebrows on snooker ball heads the pitter-patter of talk a sandwich board outside the cinema pink chalk floating hearts dotting *is* the dancing girls' dreams that levitate above their strong-hold hairspray (forget the posters of their missing faces that rot in phone booths) a dreaming young woman inside still pacing in shoes she can't walk in horror she can't shake remembering pitfalls her flushed face her boxed stare trying to escape the chance long passed glasses outside chinking in soft lilt of evening that smears itself equally even in dirt and dead-ends where peroxided blondes with kicked-in front teeth ask passing heads-down men for another chance at love or a fiver for a blowie even in alleys like these there's aphid romance even for the past-it and the henpecked for the curious lost tourist in these zones the air's younger but gone times still lurk kings crying for fox hunts *SOHO!* a myth spanning fields that were wastes urban bogs disappointment congealing into concrete apogee unmarked doorways gargling piss in acutest mornings back to the runaways laughing and slinking inside black shrouds their precocious phalanx surrounding the wooden track Terry's safety inspection went on well past dark *WHAT HAPPENS IS A DEATH-TRAP* but he couldn't quite see it just Lucy's blue and gold wild dreaming outside the cinema snoring man slumps in a parked mini-bus his cheek smooches glass waiting for men drunk with the conceit of being men for one night only dreaming from the shore he sees young sailors sung to shipwreck in blinking neon where everyone drowns in the name of light entertainment bouncers pounding gum past taste the night starting to vibrate with traffic and dropped glass the swaggering undead pronouncing themselves Sarahs Jennys nauseous Katies under coy veils waving inflatable genitals passing bouncers' winking shutters Lucy still in back room stomach ruching inside satin the sky too far above waiting its turn to speak tired Terry chinking chamomile tea with an old found burnt spoon the type scraped from dead water a florid stem weathered by heated talk in still nights a confession against a black and blue sky that Lucy wasn't seeking solace but something hard inside it Billy in dark velvet his spittle fingers stroking lapel stains he forgets their origin amid his courting days scraping dead lip near closing time watching the last dance alone in a regional club too much grease in his hair *I DON'T HAVE TIME FOR THIS SHITE* black bowtie reminding him to swallow pricked nerves pinched heels new shoes scent of stale carnations crisp to touch reminding him of mother's tuberose perfume in photos of lukewarm happiness and the camera's dim technology the second hand brings a closer scalping a truth homing in outside repeated tourist headcount someone's missing the laggard at the back has dawdled into a peep show his prescription sunglasses bouncing back darkness and its bending over his groaning grin he'll carry through security and onto the plane smoothing his face during a rocky take-off back in the cinema all shrouded teens all boned shadows spooked by a curious throng outside and prospect of speedy maths tickets for impatient punters Lucy speaking in convex mirror an endless howl glowing not quite a word forged full-bodied nonetheless painting her nude body painstakingly blue for battle a skirting reveal a taunting that will decide this place is home until razed Terry's last minute showy trims on every edge in sight chirpy flowers purfle the entrance and sparse roses saved for the stage the florist's worst at closing time romance's decay intact Billy making last minute checks flicking bugs from red seats too small for most modern bodies' gyzyming checking fire exits swabbing sweat in his creases wondering if the Duchess would approve if she's watching upstairs knocking wood for stiff luck knock-offs he'd nicked from an unsecured building site he knows he shouldn't saw off corners knows full well it'll all be fine after several stiff drinks *NO ICE I SAID NO ICE WHAT DOES IT TAKE TO GET A WARM DRINK ROUND HERE* Dave wandering up and down streets directions biroed on back of hand unsure whether he imagined the crude flyer on Lucy's computer screen the blushing giggler who couldn't make a decent cuppa he's spiked his hair higher and wears his best hoop earring in holed lobe made with unsanitized knitting needle and ice in a '70s skag squat his soprano spittles were never lived down his rank never recovered in the Contingent Lucy hugging sink and retching for dad to appear in mirror back forever from casual map audit rubbing her skin in circles she's not sure anymore how limbs work was her movement just keenness not to be found wanting are her wheels fake rhythms she can't match *HE WAS KEEPING OUR LAND SAFE* the gurgle where does it end up the wrong way down her starched face its blood funnelling to decision putting everything back into the undreamt before disappointment and monocular knowing the rabbit's silent stews in rills back home under her window *ME AND DAD ARE EXPLOSIONS TOGETHER* the shrouded chorines curiously watching the first stain-free walk-ins no macs the odd kagoole (in readiness for British summertime) in back room Lucy coaxing her foateling heart it'll soon all be over DNA vapours trailing her harsh blinks in dirty mirror Terry rubbing ovals around circles not silencing enough *THERE THERE*-ing without end coach party shuffling in the front door money-belts tight Billy's fear hatching behind drapes humans filling seats usually filled by dregs of men and their flaking Kleenex silent physical yesses followed by nodding off *MUSIC WE NEED MUSIC CREATE SOME AMBIENCE TERRY AND FAST* country singer belting out her dislike of whiskey her love of a sober dance a likely story in here Billy searching for drink an unemptied bottle oozing plump promise under chairs under coats a muttering apology the audience made to stand he flits into the projection room fumbling he finds rum and a shotgun belonging to Lucy's dad *who did he kill or maim just goes to show everyone's got a perfect murder in them was the dowsing a decoy from where the bodies were buried got to admire the brains* he knocks back drink which kicks with age stone mad he feels the shakes buckle but their echo is locked in here with him achromic ghosts work the floor the door does not budge he throttles its handle hears the song finish and Hank Williams' yodel start up *TURN THAT SHITE OFF TERRY* he yells swears bloody murder as he shoulders the door *WE'RE NOT DISHING OUT APPALACHIAN DARKNESS HERE* the blue velvet shoulder snagged into clean hang like a boxer dog's sour lip Billy swearing the wrong thing is happening again *oh god put it right just this once* he stands hip-width the gun cocked misses the handle Terry already's here the door open his work soon seamless he's a battlefield surgeon threading his needle gently under mortar roars panic over more rum finding a soft home out front orders are taken by runaways at the end of polite rows curious about traditional cuisine chicken in baskets unboxed out back outsourced from a local takeaway Billy's turn now in front of convex mirror New York cop voice out loud in his head slick Las Vegas compere who rolled with the rat-pack glamour scenting his vowels chewing hard toffee that could crack teeth into confession light erupts the little sparrow wakes and gets slid to the side of the stage protracted smoke rings bouncing off cheap spotlight never a true circle even in a newborn's meanest squint the rum pouring into Billy's knees cementing his sways as he gargles one last capful for luck and anything else that's going there's not much left here no state of matter *I WISH MAMMY COULD SEE ME NOW AND GRAHAM AND ALL THOSE LADS WHO RAN ME DOWN MY CORONATION AT LONG BLEEDIN LAST* he jabs in fast skiamachy peeks at numbers he never pictured but who's that in the shadows where the dad used to dim proceedings *BET HE SHOT THAT GUN PICKING OFF THE SLOW COMERS* Sinbad lurks there wiping his brow still confused at the beer-soaked flyer folded into slapdash origami on pub table the address could not be right surely that can't be sweet Lucy bending over surely the little sparrow didn't have it in her to turn this place around who was it what kind of mug got involved picnicked on his turf whose cash papered the cracks got rid of the dirty mac brigade the whispering tourists sat in front of him too polite too scared to ask for serviettes for greasy fingers Sinbad sees the wooden track doing the rounds some kind of cabaret he suspects Lucy rubs her gut out back still seasick at the prospect her face gone milky staying there no one knows how long til show-time Billy revving up with one extra capful shouts *GO GO GO!* dying wishing propels the skates on stage Lucy behind them lock-jawed too fast vicious body seized in desperate balance she roars through red drapes advancing through fat wooden heart satin clasps her body shaking in prisms taunting the paying eye the little donkey Sphinxes gin-ganging the room Billy hand-wringing in the wings Lucy's minatory Charleston raking fear and piecemeal claps to curt silence next sequence sloppy rumba round houses but she'll recover curving air in swoops she travels over heads *SHIT!* she nearly misses first corner *concentrate* her wheels pressing into wood rickety grit to keep going despite god and dad and the dealt card mother smoking a storm the little engine that could runaways' drumming translating earthquakes into pidgin English languaged weather speak which eats up time and stalls it when real talk runs out Sinbad makes marble fists *WHERE'S THAT BLOODY DOG WHEN YOU NEED HIM* Lucy swoops on stage amid smoke back into draped pudenda with all her bones' grins intact relief bayouing Dave leads the whoops *STILL WATERS EH, STILL WATERS! GO ON MY GIRL* whoops again then stops when he remembers his soprano shame everything is solvable for Billy as he saunters into spotlight that stencils his ageing unkindly everything dragging gets drop-kicked his rightful place is here with a knowing jig for laughs he forgets his bad leg's dead weight a perfect score tonight his sweat's pregnant luminescence he tries to budge the microphone stand which won't so he stoops and begins *WELL,* and continues *WELL, WELL, WELL* beaming with balmy smiling pausing in a bask that's all his *WHAT A BEAUTIFUL AUDIENCE WE HAVE HERE TONIGHT.* Mad Sinbad's temper twigging behind mad-eyed flexing at the man blurred in velvet blue *I'M SO PLEASED YOU ALL COULD JOIN US FOR THE FIRST IN A SERIES OF EXTRAVAGANZAS* flighty jazz fingers pluvial joy that fills unscripted with the rum's coursing *OR SHOULD I SAY EXTRAVAGINAS HA I'M SO PROUD OF THE ENTERTAINMENT WE HAVE IN STORE FOR YOU TONIGHT WHAT YOU'VE SEEN IS JUST A TASTE* his sways calming one eye lazes the grip on the mic stand a rueful weighing Sinbad appalled nail digging dark for red dead-animal breath Billy promising not to run the sound of the child-lock opening *look Sinbad my hands are tied I won't get very far* bolting into lightlessness they drove for hours no horizon in sarcastic serein amid landfill piles the stench spilling with tiredness the gulls' metal laughs above rust Billy's whereabouts hiding in rubbish tunnelling escape or dead under scrap and arson guilt now trying to ruin him again to rub his face in old ash *AND THAT GIRL ON WHEELS ISN'T SHE BRILLIANT WELL THAT'S NOT THE LAST YOU'VE SEEN OF HER TONIGHT NO LADIES AND GENTS SHE'S THE STAR OF OUR SHOW SOON TO BE A NEW WEST END SENSATION MY SNOW ANGEL ROLLERSKATING LUCY* the girl's name's a gulped fist *VIRGIN TALENT UNDISCOVERED TIL NOW IT'S A PLEASURE TO SHARE HER WITH YOU TONIGHT LADIES AND GENTS ALTHOUGH I DO WISH I COULD KEEP HER ALL TO MYSELF HUR HUR YOU KNOW WHAT I MEAN OR YOU SOON WILL STAY WHERE YOU ARE LADIES AND GENTS IT'S GONNA GET RACIER AND RACIER AND I DON'T JUST MEAN THE ROLLERSKATING* blood bulldozes wrong way seeing red after red and the rest is muffled *I'VE HAD THE PRIVELEGE TO WATCH HER GROW INTO A STAR SHE TRULY IS SOMETHING SPECIAL*

AND YOU'LL BE TELLING EVERYONE ABOUT TONIGHT SO MAKE SURE YOU BRING THEM WITH YOU ON YOUR NEXT VISIT FOR A COMPLIMENTARY SHOESHINE IT REALLY HAS BEEN A JOURNEY FOR THE BOTH OF US YOU KNOW SORRY TO GET SENTIMENTAL BUT IT'S BEEN TOUGH GOING FOR ME THESE LAST FEW YEARS BUT I CAN FEEL THE LOVE IN THIS ROOM AND I'M JUST SO THRILLED TO BE HERE SHOWCASING SUCH AMAZING BEAUTY AND TALENT SO LET'S GET HER OUT HERE TO SAY HELLO COME ON LOVELY LUCY DON'T BE SHY sulky child in nativity play fondles loose hem ISN'T SHE LOVELY LADIES AND GENTS SUCH A SWEET GIRL YOUTH'S BLOOM SO WELL PROPORTIONED I'M SO PROUD OF HER Sinbad moving up aisle his shadow's jealous hulk stains wall ANYWAY THAT'S ENOUGH OF ME GABBING ON LET'S SEE SOME SNATCH ON WHEELS EH THAT'S WHY WE'RE HERE Sinbad now on stage his body swaying ping-ponging heated asides Billy oblivious still falling in love Sinbad's hands on the mic stand squeaking it to full height GOOD EVENING LADIES AND GENTS SORRY TO INTERRUPT PROCEEDINGS BUT I AM THE OWNER OF THIS ESTABLISHMENT YOU MAY HAVE SEEN ME ON TELEVISION BUT UNFORTUNATELY THAT'S NOT WHY I'M HERE TONIGHT ALTHOUGH I DO HAVE SOME EXCITING REALITY PROJECTS IN THE PIPELINE THIS MAN HERE IS A FUGITIVE AND I'LL BE MAKING A CITIZEN'S ARREST ON STAGE smattering claps SORRY FOR ANY INCONVENIENCE TO YOUR EVENING'S ENTERTAINMENT BUT I CAN HIGHLY RECOMMEND THE PERFECT PUSSY CLUB ON WARDOUR STREET IF YOU WISH TO CONTINUE IT FURTHER Billy snatches it back the end is now small print Lucy's mother's engine flagging her butt bouquet drooping onto drapes' trims Lucy impatient behind curtain kegel exercising the moon shining among lesser fires Sinbad snatches the microphone back *NOT ONLY IS THIS MAN AN ARSONIST HE'S A DANGEROUS FANTASIST* Billy's tarantist twitches their useless big reveal *UNLESS YOU'RE IN IT TOGETHER EH THE PAIR OF YOU CARRYING ON BEHIND MY BACK* mother's tiny flames creep from the back inching into scene soon diluvial considered part of the show *I'M SORRY, I'M SORRY, I'M SORRY* Billy kneading his lapels for teleportation or plain waking all pasts and futures still contenders in here *JUST LET HER DANCE PLEASE* mother up in smoke a grinning monk an all-seeing scream Terry rolls her in aggressive carpet virusing Billy and Sinbad eye-balling rolling their sleeves for tough work prepping for throned wounds Terry sighing clocking-in taking control *PLEASE COULD EVERYONE LEAVE THEIR SEATS IN AN ORDERLY MANNER NO RUNNING OR PUSHING PLEASE* Sinbad butting in *YOU COULDN'T HELP YOURSELF BILLY YOU HAD TO BURN DOWN YOUR DREAMS COS YOU KNOW THEY'RE BUILT ON BUGGER ALL* the front row in flames *LUCY WE HAVE TO STOP* the girl eager for her heart circus to stop here for the night

I HAVEN'T DONE MY BIG NUMBER YET IT'S FOR DAD

WHAT ABOUT YOUR DAD?

HE'S JUDGING MY DANCE ON THE FRONT ROW

YOUR DAD CROAKED YOU DAFT COW YOU LOT DESERVE EACH OTHER YOU'RE ALL GONE WITH THE

*BLEEDIN' FAIRIES YOU'RE DOING ME A FAVOUR
GUTTING THIS PLACE BILLY BRING ON THE BOUTIQUE
APARTMENTS*

Lucy's death-stagger into sombre kneel chorines like clockwork sprint on stage holding back edges of blackness assembling Neolithic calyx herd etching grief down their cheeks Lucy crumbling as ache sings desiderium *ALAS, ALAS, WOE, WOE! DADDY'S HERE WATCHING I CAN SEE HIM DRINKING WHISKEY ON THE ROCKS OVER THERE SHIPWRECKED AND SMILING AND I'M THE ONLY ONE SINGING* chorines slowly tearing shrouds beating breasts the same wordless rhythm that punctures with toothy anguish *ee, oa, totoi, popoi!* tourist evacuees pausing to hear girls' quavering sa-yelema unutterable horse-power Lucy's rough therapy rocking clapping mad at heart and bone her head bowed body compact back into young flatness ready for tough warring ever announcing thunder indoors hymns fit for hell's worst rooms Terry shrugging at Billy who's lifting a fire extinguisher trying to read instructions without glasses metallic taste of death mattering as brash quality Lucy seeing constellations bigger than cities *I WILL BURN MY CLOTHES AND FIND MY DAD THOUGH GRIEF PECKS AT MY EYES* blue body sordid leaking shimmying darkness merging together against narrow flame:

Otototototototototototototototo to
totototototot totototototototot t
otototototot totototototototot
totototototot totototototototot
totototototot totototototototot
totototototot totototototototot
totototototot totototototototot
totototototot totototototototot
totototototot totototototototot
totototototot totototototototot
totototototot totototototototot
totototototot totototototototot
totototototot totototototototot
totototototot totototototototot
totototototot totototototototot
totototototot totototototototot
totototototot totototototototot
totototototot totototototototot
totototototot totototototototot
totototototot totototototototot
totototototot totototototototo
t totototototot totototototot
ot totototototot totototototo
tot totototototot totototoi!

TERRY SHE'S HAVING A FIT GET HER OFF THE STAGE THIS IS NOT PART OF THE ACT Terry shushes Billy closes the doors the wind's changed for good now its minor key infarcted but still wheezing its wrongs and fears keen to leak into night into witness statements into small talk of the past the wrong thing said these tides don't turn that moon long gone but still breathing down your neck thirsty problems leading them to water under blanket night Lucy's skin growing taller bad weeds stalagmited mascara curdling with each kick a dead angle hot to touch lacunulose daddy smiles from the front row in her wet squint he's foot-tapping and squeezing a pint glass the old banned type that brains men in unfair pub fights the audience back levitating briefly above seats fumbling for expensive cameras *HE WILL NOT BE BURIED UNWEPT AND UNWATERED* Lucy's slip shedded while Sinbad drags Billy into damp alley the old humiliation cranks up against wall the sailor reaching into monographed sock for letter opener's sultry glint it's a quick learner and knower of hearts it births dark continent on ironed pale ocean breeching all horizons Sinbad's eyes now obsidian beads of calm *HAVE YOU SEEN HIM HAVE YOU SEEN HIM* a wretched wading spreading her legs inside *I WILL I WILL I WILL* Lucy sessile to stage insensate to hereness *DADDY WAS FOREVER* she climbs up into flame-licked beams dust coating her bloodied breast away from the runaways away from wire mother away from the dolmen *WHO WANTS TO SEE ME FUCKED OR DEAD I WANT NO CLAQUES NO PLEUREURS IN HERE GET BACK AND GIVE ME YOUR SCORES* Terry second-guesses stands underneath his orant arms waiting for her *NOW YOU MUST GO*

DAD HOW WILL I COPE DAD I MUST GO TOO DAD discovery of voice by animal in death giving inch to dad's placelessness no call no response lifted from murk a false remembering *BURY ME INSTEAD* refusal to carry skin a woman's body no more never again it crackles and spits then mere silence amid heat after comes worse healing in a bed by a tall window (mother still living sometimes percolating with rawness she forgot plenty parking her frame in a nursing home blocking TV cliff-hangers making residents cry no one likes having to guess endings to move on with missing parts) Lucy knows this on a well-lit ward where no fresh flowers are allowed the slow drip revving the bleed of a warm shawl kissing her eschars her thick smell iron-rich dressed daily she is stalled somewhere in Edenic green comparing her small hand to a long afternoon the pain sanded to gentle plateau mum has made lemonade and yells she'll give it to the dog if I don't come back and I laugh when I watch him bite ice and think about dog years human years lights years and what's secret what's never said remember dad says mind the stinging nettles on your chicken legs sometimes we find coloured eggs he says not to touch them or the mum won't come back and this makes me cry how Roy Orbison sings cry